KISS OF THE WOLF

KISS
OF THE
WOLF

Jim Shepard

Harcourt Brace & Company

New York   San Diego   London

Requests for permission to make copies of any
part of the work should be mailed to:
Permissions Department, Harcourt Brace & Company,
6277 Sea Harbor Drive, Orlando, Florida 32887-6777.

Library of Congress Cataloging-in-Publication Data
Shepard, Jim.
Kiss of the wolf/Jim Shepard.—1st ed.
p.   cm.
ISBN 0-15-147279-3
I. Title.
PS3569.H39384K57   1994
813'.52—dc20   93-31467

Designed by Lydia D'moch

Printed in the United States of America

First edition

A B C D E

for Aidan

KISS OF THE WOLF

JOANIE

WE ARE RESPONSIBLE for the bad things that happen to us. My best friend during my two years of college, Mary Mucci, she used to say that all the time. Her boyfriend was a Christian Scientist—we all have our crosses to bear—and he talked like that. Her mother had a stroke, her little sister drank, and she developed this spinal thing, and the way they saw it, she wasn't off the hook for any of it.

When I told my mother that Gary was history, the first thing she said was, Oh, my God, come over here, bring Todd, stay the night. The second thing she said was, What'd you do?

I took a week off at school. They understood. Nancy covered some of my classes. It was like maternity leave: abandonment leave. For a few weeks I was excused as lay reader at the church.

I talked to Father Cleary. My mother's idea. I told

him the same thing I told her. I had no idea, this woman's name had never come up, things had been more or less fine between us. Shock to Joanie. Out of the blue. You think you know someone, etc.

The lies I told them are the lies I tell myself.

So now I sit at my desk and go through my address book. It's not a pretty sight. Whole letters of the alphabet are empty. Not just *Q*'s and *X*'s, either. Where're the *F*'s? Where're the *J*'s? I don't know anyone whose name begins with *J*? Some letters have, like, on a whole page, one uncle listed. I sit here with a new daily planner, amazed at the white space.

Shopping, sitting around, going to Mass, I feel pitiful. I should: I look pitiful. I'm heavier, got circles under my eyes. When I went back to school to finish the year, my kids knew. Every day was agony. I was being pitied by high school kids. Even now I get looks, like I'm walking around with a sign that says, I'm alone, I'm unhappy, don't be mean to me.

Now it's like people see me and say, What's the *opposite* of envy?

I've gone out a little since. Though then I feel guilty: that's even less time with Todd. He's still a kid, and even on the best days he's alone most of the time. I'm not the kind of mom to sit him down for a heart-to-heart over a plate of sugar cookies. Now he's getting his father's talent for shifting rooms to avoid people. Somebody comes over, he's like a ghost: whatever room you're in, he's not. Sometimes I imagine a light like a little moon that won't let us stray too far apart, a safety light he can carry in the dark when he's alone.

What do I say to him that'll help, that he can take with him, that'll save him from trouble? What kind of advice that he wouldn't formulate for himself?

What do I offer in place of his father?

Sometimes I want to get out and away from everything so much I think about a time Todd was playing outside and the dog couldn't get to him, was stuck inside with me, and the way she stood there and would not give up, the way she gave me, over and over, that pure, insistent whine and that look at the door, like that was *all she wanted*.

I'm Catholic. I still have the little Nativity scenes and peekaboo Blessed Virgins from the spelling bees. When I don't sin, I forget all about it. When I do, I remember.

The family's helped. My mother, too, though she's a pain in the ass. I feel bad for her. She keeps at it, keeps up her end, manages to have fun, even though the way she sees it, life's a series of setups and disappointments. You can tell from the way she looks at things: the house, the addition they never put on, my father. Poor Nina's family is too good-natured, pays its bills on time, never cuts corners, always grabs for the check, gets kicked in the ass for its trouble. Poor Nina just makes things worse for herself. And it's true: it annoys her that she annoys people. She's mostly sad, but her sadness reminds everybody else of hostility. When she says to me, Your father's too good-hearted, it doesn't sound anything like a compliment. I'm one of my mother's disappointments, too, now. I'm just beginning to realize that.

NINA

I GIVE HER CREDIT. She's married twelve years, she finds a note—a *corner* of another piece of paper, she showed it to me—under the dial thing on the phone. They have to make new arrangements, he'll call from out west. She said to me when she told me, "Ma, new arrangements."

What do you do? The house was paid for and she had the job at the school. No one was going to starve. So what do you do? Help her out, little things here and there. Get her to get a lawyer after him. For a few weeks they ate over. I cooked extras, lasagna, stew, you could freeze it, it'd keep for a while. We cleaned. She was never one for a clean house, but she wanted his stuff *out*. He wrote a letter from wherever he was, said he'd send for his things. She said he could send for whatever he liked, it'd all be out on the street. Which is where it went. She had boxes full of his crap on the curb. Bicycle outfits, sweaters, magazines, pictures in frames, baseball gloves. When you looked into the box, you saw things like playing cards and rings at the bottom. It was hard on Todd, so we tried to get her to stop, but she got wild, so we gave up. Todd sat on the front porch and watched her lug stuff out until Sandro made him come inside. Before he went, he took a few things out of the boxes, to keep. Sandro let it go. What are you going to do: take things out of the kid's hands?

People in cars came from all over Connecticut, stopped and poked around and picked out what they wanted. Maybe two people came to the house to see if it was all right. We pleaded with her to save some stuff or at least have a tag sale, but forget it, she didn't want to hear it. Some wedding stuff she left in the attic. That was it. Finally Sandro took three boxes of what was left to the Salvation Army. Todd was so upset watching it go that I felt bad for Sandro.

It was a sin.

You just try and convince everybody it's not the end of the world.

You feel bad for the kid. What's he know? What's he supposed to make of all this? And for her.

She says, "Ma, I feel bad for *you*. This's all been hard on you." That's the kind of heart she's got. I tell her we all have our crosses to bear. Her father and I were lucky: she never got into drugs, did okay in school. Was never too wild. The Ciufolos, they were dealing whatever they were dealing years before they got caught. Now their mother visits them up in Danbury prison. And poor Mrs. Palasino, she's raising a grandson, the parents took off.

Joanie's husband wasn't gone two days, Bruno Minea was over here, asking how she was. Mr. Bacigalupe, I call him. I said she was fine, thanks, and however she was, she wasn't receiving visitors. She's pretty, she's still got her looks, so every *ragazzo* in town's gotta sniff around, and every one of them thinks, you know, this is damaged goods, anyway. It's like I told her: in Filene's Basement you don't handle the clothes the way you do upstairs. We were over the DeFeos'; Bruno sat next to her the whole time. He's had his eye on her twenty years; twenty years he hasn't had a good thought about her. They go back all the way to Blessed Sacrament. You see the look on his face around her we used to see from the dogs around the butcher's. I told her, with him sitting right there, just like my mother told me: when he's talking to you, you keep a *volto sciolto pensiero stretto*—an open face and a closed mind.

For a while she was feeling better. So what does she do? Her husband tells her to fly to Chicago, they need to talk. She flies to Chicago. Todd was up all night, every night. He stayed with us. Every five minutes: when were we gonna hear? Sandro almost went out of his mind. So they talked, nothing happened, she came home. The poor kid, he was a wreck. Joanie didn't say anything for a few days, then she came over, sat with me here in the kitchen, and cried. She said, "Ma, what'd I do wrong? What'd I do?"

I didn't say anything. But I wanted to tell her this story I remembered, from back in Italy: this guy worked the land for this baroness and lived a long way from her. One day she sent for him, said she wanted to see him. So he walks this whole way to see her, and when he gets to the gates of the villa, there she is, way off by the house. And she makes a sign for him to stop where he is. And she looks at him through this telescope she has, just looks at him, him standing there at the gate holding his hat. Then she waves her hand, bye-bye, bye-bye, and sends him away.

TODD

MY DOG'S NAME is Audrey. She's half Irish setter, half beagle. When we tell people that, they always look at us like, half what and half what? But she is. She's a little bigger than a beagle, and her coat's red like an Irish setter's. My dad got her for us, upstate. He named her after Audrey Meadows from "The Honeymooners." She was free. She's nine years old. She had growths on her side, but the vet said they didn't mean anything. He cut one off. She has white hairs on her muzzle, from stress.

I want to go to lacrosse camp this year, but I probably won't. My mom doesn't even know I want to go. I don't have a stick or anything, but I borrowed a friend's and really liked it. I watched the NCAA championships on TV. Princeton won. I was rooting for Syracuse.

School's been over for two weeks. In gym we did

crab ball, which was good but hurt your hands. We finished gymnastics. I was good on the rope climb, once I got used to the way it swayed near the top. I was a star on the springboard. I was best on the pommel horse. I sucked on the uneven parallel bars. Which is a girl's thing.

I live alone with my mother.

We see a lot of my mother's parents—Nina and Sandro, I call them. My friends say, God, you call your grandparents that? I go, Yeah. That's their names. My father's parents we hardly ever see. I guess they're ashamed.

When my dad left, he left a note on the phone. That was it. He mighta snuck into my room and said good-bye or something, but I don't know. I'm a light sleeper. He sent me a letter that was two pages long once he got out to Colorado, but it was not real informative. I sent him back this card I made of Audrey flying an F-16 and hanging a paw out the canopy. Audrey was saying, "WHEN ARE YOU COMING BACK?" He wrote and thanked me like that wasn't a serious question.

The day I got his letter I watched cable twenty-three straight hours, nine in the morning to eight in the morning, still my record. My mom was a wreck. I saw the strangest ending to any movie ever. The movie was called *Half Angel*. There's a good gangster and a bad gangster. At the end the good gangster goes to kiss the girl, and right in the middle of it his friend starts this gross story about this other gangster who kills everybody. His friend goes, "Yeah, Bugs himself was drooling with the lust of slaughter." That's exactly what he said, and the movie ends like that. I watched it twice, at 1:00 A.M. and 4:00 A.M., because I couldn't believe it.

A few weeks after my father left, my mother and I had a fight. We had more fights than that, but this was a big one. I broke about seven things in my room, and my mother kicked open the door. She broke the lock. It was like martial arts or something. Later she said, "When did you ever have it so bad? What did we ever do to you?" So I said, "Okay," and told her about the time we went to Moodus Lake to look at the property they bought and never did anything with. We went there like once every three years to prove to ourselves we still had it. We never used it. Where our part was, the water was all weedy and gross, like a swamp, and there was no driveway in—you had to walk through the woods—and not even a good place to camp. We all went up there, and they went off to talk to the owner of the land association or somebody and told me to lock the doors and not let anybody in and wait where I was. Where was I going? We were pulled off this dirt road in the middle of the woods. One side of the car had like smashed branches up against the windows. I just sat there. They couldn't find him. It was like they were gone forever. Then they couldn't find the car. They took the wrong trail or something. It got dark. I was in the backseat. I had the radio on. I thought it'd be good for them if I ran the battery down, and then I thought that was stupid, because we'd all be stuck here when they got back. Even so, I left it on. And the disc jockey or whoever must've put a stack of records on the turntable and gone away, because something stuck, and the station played "Down in the Boondocks" like fifty times in a row. The guy announced it once, and then it just kept coming on. I couldn't believe it. I couldn't change the station or turn it off. I kept thinking the next time the guy would come in and stop it. I wanted to see if he'd apologize, or what. I don't know what happened. Finally I got too scared for the battery and turned it off. I could still hear the song in my head. It was pitch-black, and there were all these cricket sounds and rustlings. I spent some time closing my eyes and checking out those circles and gray things that float around behind your eyelids. I thought, They don't even have a flash-light. The song coming back was worse than the sound of the woods: Down in the Boondocks. I sang it, though that was the last thing I wanted to do: " 'People put me down 'cause that's the side of town I was born in. I love her, she loves me, but I don't fit in her society.' " Then I heard them calling, and I turned on the headlights, and they found me.

BRUNO

THREE GUYS walk into a bar. Roof collapses, kills 'em all. Turns out they had cancer.

Hard Luck stories. Poor Me stories. Isn't It Sad stories. *Isn't it sad I had to do what I had to do?* I looked the other way during kickbacks, I put less in the Sunday envelope, I hit my kid and now he's got this stutter, my husband left me, and I had to raise my three blind girls alone. Bruno, Bruno, poor Elena, poor Lucia, poor whoever, poor me, no one should have this much trouble. Bruno, Bruno, you're so hardhearted. Isn't it sad? I say, You got trouble? Too bad, my condolences, *deal* with it. There's no trick to this. I'm not here as a therapist. This guy Darwin on TV had it right: you got too many legs, a fin out to here, teeth smaller than Harvey across the rock, you're not gonna make it. And what is that? What? Bad *luck?* You pray all your *life* you don't get luck like some people get. Guys with no eyes, guys whose whole families go down on some boat, guys who're vegetables, get fed off a tray. People say, Bruno you wouldn't be so hard it happened to you—I say, My father came over here, he was fourteen years old, knew four words of English—four—worked on the highways going in upstate for three days and a back-loader dumped a load of shale where he was standing, crushed his legs. Guy called, "All clear?" and my dad waved and stood there. My mother died of this simple thing because some Mick doctor couldn't find his ass with both hands and a diagram. I'm forty-two years old, never got married, I've gone broke twice. Started up from nothing twice. Now I sell cars. You think I *like* selling cars? My life is a bowl of *roses* selling cars?

I came here, started working in the off-season. Everything was down. Sales were down. The economy was down. Inventory was down. Spirits were down, morale was down, the shade in my office was down. The desk they gave me, the drawers didn't open. They probably figured, Guinea, he's not gonna write anything, anyway. They told me I couldn't use the coffee machine. I hadda go across the street. You imagine this? Bruno, it's only an eight-cupper. Oh, I didn't *realize*. You know what it's like, you're humping to sell the car, Gee, Mr. Dickhead, would you like a cuppa coffee? Okay, well, we'll have to go across the street, see, because I got this *disease* and they don't let me touch their fucking coffeepot. Gas shortage, oil shortage, money shortage, no beans for the soup: just the time to be selling ocean-liner Buicks in Bridgeport. I'm brand new at this, standing there in my—I got one suit, I change the shirt and ties day to day—and guys're coming in without a pot to piss in, just looking for transportation, and I'm pushing station wagons with power sunroofs. Four doors you can land planes on. The whole world's selling little Nip cars to Yupsters at eighty-percent markups and I'm selling V-8s to cane-dragging Sanka-sucking cottontops. But I sold. I sold to everybody. I sold to morons. I sold to kids. I sold to widows with bad eyesight. I sold to sharpies. I sold to Puerto Ricans. I sold to *mulignons*. I sold to family. I got my coffeepot. I drink their coffee now.

You don't think I cut corners? You don't think I did what I had to, to move inventory? You don't think I *lied* to people? You don't think I *cheated* people? Before we had a name for it, before we called it anything, we did it.

So now I hear, Bruno, you been lucky. You been doing good lately. Lately, kiss my ass lately.

Bruno, you're not for her, leave her alone, she's had too much trouble.

Listen to this: I am the guy for her. I am the guy.

Bruno, she lost her husband. Hey, she lost her husband. Worse: the guy ran off and left her. She's alone in the world. She's gotta raise the kid by herself. It's tough. Bruno, she doesn't need you around, complicating things. I told her what the loan sharks used to tell *me* on Kissuth Street: Hey, I'm not here to *observe* your problem. I'm here to *enlarge* it.

Joanie and I go back to when we were kids on North Avenue. We go back to Blessed Sacrament. Years later, I told her I was the guy, when we were still kids. She put her hand right up to touch your mouth when you were talking. You could taste her.

What do I want from her? What are my *intentions* toward her? The days I don't see her, the days I don't hear about her, I draw her picture on the wall.

PART ONE

Todd was getting confirmed. Confirmation made him an adult in the eyes of the Church. At the ceremony, Joanie tried to remember her own confirmation but couldn't. She squatted in the pew and thought dull and repetitive things like, Do I really have a son old enough to be confirmed? The bishop read Todd's name out of sequence, the only mistake he made all day. Back at home, Todd changed into play clothes and took off for parts unknown while Joanie napped away the rest of the afternoon. The whole thing seemed like an official transition to something more unpleasant.

They still had to deal with Todd's confirmation party that night. Joanie's mother was having it at her house: more room, she said. They got there early to help, and while Joanie dumped antipasto from plastic tubs onto a silver tray Nina saw a mouse under the refrigerator. This was the end of the world. They all had to hunt for the mouse. Together with Sandro they moved the refrigerator, banged around under the cabinets. Todd, of course, thought they should let it go. Nina, while she set the table, stayed upset about the mouse; for her it was One More Thing.

Once everybody showed up, Todd got a watch, a cableknit sweater, and some envelopes. His father's present had come in the mail a week early, no return address. There was a card taped to it made of a folded piece of paper. It said on the top, "Sorry to Miss the Festivities." Todd hadn't shown her the inside.

It was a small party. Nancy, her mother, Elena, and Joanie's great-aunt Clorinda, so old she never said anything. Sandro, Nina, Todd, Joanie, and the mouse. Like all Italian parties, it was planned for all rooms and stayed in the kitchen. Nina started them on the antipasto Joanie'd done a lousy job of arranging, and some spinach bread. The antipasto was good, but the spinach in the spinach bread wasn't chopped up enough. Joanie worked on a piece for minutes. Todd sat around picking at things and waiting for his father's phone call.

Everyone knew his father was supposed to be calling.

Joanie was spear carrier. Her mother was throwing the party, her son was guest of honor, her missing husband the offstage star. At one point her mother served more coffee by leaning in front of her while she was talking, like she was the ghost nobody could see.

Everyone ate the olives and left the marinated vegetables. They lined olive pits up on their dishes like hotels in Monopoly. The spinach bread wasn't going over. Sandro suggested Todd start the present-opening.

Todd looked over the pile and opened Joanie's first. A lightweight jacket for school. Purple and gold, Nike. He liked it, she thought. She'd had little energy to pick something out and had decided, anyway, not to play "Can You Top This?" with her husband's mystery gift. Todd waited one or two presents more before pulling his father's and a few others closer. That self-restraint constricted some part of her chest.

Nina, meanwhile, went ahead with the mouse hunt. She had that look, like every part of her life had come apart and she wasn't waiting any longer on *this* one. Sandro wanted to know what kind of *cavone* went exterminating when she had guests. He told her to get up and got on his hands and knees in her place, clunking around under the cabinets with a broom.

Gary's present sat there, the one everyone wanted opened, until Sandro, sweating and peeved, pulled his head out from under the sink and said, "Hey, open your father's."

"Shut up, Sandro, why don't you," Nina said. "Let him open what he wants to open."

Sandro stood up and stretched, his hand on the small of his back. He was bald and the white hairs on top of his head waved like undersea plants.

"You get it?" Nina said, meaning the mouse.

"You mind if I take a leak?" he said. He went into the bathroom. On the way out, he made a stop at the stereo in the living room. Lou Monte came on. "Pepino the Italian Mouse": "The other night I called my girl, I asked her could we meet. I said, Let's go to my house, we could have a bite to eat. But as she walked in through the door, she screamed at a-whadda she saw: there was little Pepino doin' a cha-cha on the floor."

Everyone around the table was quiet. Todd had his hands on his father's gift. Elena chewed with her mouth closed. Sandro came back from the living room. Joanie heard a skittering under the cabinet and imagined the mouse trying to get a look, too.

The present was in a square, head-sized box. The day it arrived, Todd wandered in and out of the kitchen, where they'd left it, checking it out from all angles. Now he had one hand on top of it, as if to see if it was warm. He pulled it closer. The sliding sound on the tablecloth reminded her of moving boxes, moving in.

The phone rang. Joanie answered it. Someone for Bruno. Whoever it was, he sounded pretty unhappy. While Joanie talked to him Nina put a hand to her collarbone and threw Joanie a "That was close" look. Joanie crossed her eyes at her. Todd started working on the box.

It was sealed with some sort of clear supertape. Nina got scissors.

The phone rang again, this time for Joanie. She sighed and took it around the corner, with a finger in her ear. It was Bruno: something'd come up, he'd be a little late. Joanie wanted to say, We care. When she got off, the box was open. Todd was holding the thing up.

It turned out to be a lacrosse helmet. He was controlling his face, but she could see he loved it, absolutely loved it.

"Oh, that's lovely," Sandro said. Everyone was doing their "Great gift" murmurs.

"What is it?" Nina said, like they'd found it under a rock.

"It's a lacrosse helmet," Sandro said. "Don't you know nothing?"

"No, I don't know nothing," Nina said. "I should know an across helmet?"

"It's sports," Sandro said.

"Pardon me," Nina said. "I thought it was olive picking."

Todd didn't try it on. He was holding it by the facemask. He loved lacrosse and had wanted something like this for months; she could see it in his face. Before this second she would have been as likely to say he was interested in the Flags of All Nations, or dolls.

Eleven years old: wasn't that too young for lacrosse? Where'd he hear about lacrosse? Who played it?

Things were awkward for a while. No one knew how enthusiastic to be. Nina refilled coffees.

It took Todd some time to get to the next present. Nancy finally said, "You gonna open mine, or what?" and he set the helmet in his lap and looked over what was left. Nancy pointed hers out.

A line had formed for the bathroom. Sandro picked up the lacrosse helmet and squeezed it onto his head.

"Don't play around, you're gonna stretch it," Nina said. She was broiling sausage and peppers. She had to check on them nineteen times, and Sandro had to move his chair every time she did.

"What 'stretch it'?" Sandro said. "It's plastic."

Nina asked him if he was through with the mouse. Was she going to have to hire someone, thirty-fi' dollars an hour? Sandro ignored her.

Joanie took time out to track her feelings, like a little weather map. At this point she was hoping her husband wouldn't call. She wanted it unanimous, what everyone thought of him. She wanted it consistent the way he treated everyone. She looked at Todd and his bad haircut and the little Band-Aid that wouldn't stick on his hand and was surprised, the way she was always surprised, not by her own meanness but by its persistence.

Sandro got back on his hands and knees with a Mother of God sigh and clacked around under the sink again with the broom handle. It was like he was trying to warn the mouse, not catch it. Nancy poured Joanie more wine, then sat back and made fun of her vacant expression.

Joanie woke up and nodded. Nancy pointed to her gift, finally about to be unwrapped. Todd was working on it like it was a bomb.

"You don't have to save the paper," Nancy said. "Really."

She was Joanie's best friend. Joanie hadn't talked to her at all about Gary's leaving, and it had been two months. Nancy would come over and they'd go to a movie, split a Greek salad. Once, early on, Joanie had been crying upstairs, and Nancy sat in the kitchen and waited a half hour and then finally went home.

Todd was holding up her gift: a book called *Italian Folktales.*

"Oh, a book," Nina said flatly. No one seemed to know what to make of her tone. Nancy taught at Stratford High with Joanie—English and history—and liked to give Todd books.

"See if there are any stories about Mucherinos in there," Sandro said.

"That's in the famous-crime-stories book," Nancy said.

"Take that off," Nina said. "You're sweating in it."

"I need this for the mouse," Sandro said.

The phone rang again. Sandro got it, in the lacrosse helmet. He clacked the plastic receiver against his earhole and kept going, "*Hel*lo? Hel*lo?*" like it was a vaudeville routine. It got a laugh.

He said, "Joanie, it's Bruno," and handed her the phone. Joanie gave Nancy her "I'm not encouraging this" look.

Nancy had gone out with Bruno for a little while, high school and afterward. She still had a thing for him. She was sitting here hoping *he* wouldn't call.

We're all sitting around hoping guys won't call, Joanie thought.

"What's up?" she said into the phone. "You hit another snag?"

"I'm on my way over," Bruno said. Something was being whacked behind him.

"What is that?" Joanie said.

"I don't know," Bruno said. "They're screwing around. I'm over here by the deli. You want me to bring anything?"

"We got everything," Joanie said. "You're missing all the presents being opened."

"I was over here, you know, I thought I'd call, see if you needed something," Bruno said. "I'm five minutes away."

"What's that noise behind you?" Joanie said.

"I don't know, these fucking guys," Bruno said. The line went muffled, as if he'd covered the mouthpiece with his hand, and when he uncovered it, the sound was gone.

Joanie shifted her weight. Todd was opening more presents. Somebody'd given him some kind of board game he wouldn't play in a thousand years. "So you coming?" Joanie said in her "I'm getting off" voice.

"Tell 'im we got the Great Mouse Hunt goin'

over here," Sandro said. He was whisking around under the stove now.

"Listen. Nancy there?" Bruno said.

"Yes, she is," Joanie said. Nancy looked up at her. "Wanna talk to her?"

"Don't bust 'em off," Bruno said. "Her mother there?"

"Yes, she is," Joanie said. Elena was over by the door, hadn't said two words all night. "You wanna talk to her?"

"Yeah, give her a message for me," Bruno said. "Tell her, *'Mangia il gatz.'* "

"You tell her," Joanie said.

"I'm on my way," Bruno said. He hung up.

She came back to the table and sat down. Nancy was looking at her. Joanie shrugged.

"Where's the dog?" Nina said, like she'd just noticed the dog wasn't around. "Why didn't you bring the dog?" She was probably thinking of the mouse.

"She ran away again," Joanie said.

Audrey'd had a tough last few months and had taken to running away after dinner for a few hours. Todd would go look for her, stand in the yard and wait for her to come back.

Nina turned the peppers, which had to be done by now. "That dog's gonna be out in the woods, she's gonna be running around, she's gonna get bit, she's gonna get rabbis," she said.

"That's *rabies*," Sandro said. "Jesus God. *Rabies*."

Nancy laughed. Nina was used to it. Her husband said she butchered the language like Leo Gorcey. Bruno said she had her own way of communicating, and it didn't work.

"You are something," Sandro said. "The other day she goes to me, talking about that poor *chiboni* who hit the kid, 'Oh, baby. Nothing goes right for him. He's got an albacore around his neck.' "

More people laughed, even Elena. "Nice image," Nancy said.

"You believe how fast they go on that curve?" Nina said. "Three times the car flipped. These people and that curve, it's a sin."

"I think the parents are now ascared the guy's gonna get sued," Sandro said.

"I'd sue 'im," Nina said. "Three times the car flipped. They had to get that thing and tear the roof off to get him out."

"The kid was just walking there, too," Elena said from over by the door. "Going to get ice cream. You believe that? It's a shame."

"Her eyes're open now," Sandro said. "Her mother's there every day, soon as the hospital opens."

31

He had his helmeted head on the floor next to the stove, and he seemed to think he saw something.

"*Three times* that car flipped," Nina said.

"I went there and visited," Elena said. "You go?"

"I went there the second day, with the mother," Nina said. "You believe the perfume she wears? I think she marinates in it."

"Ma," Joanie said. "How about giving her a break? Her daughter's a vegetable."

"Don't talk that way," Nina said.

Joanie felt bad she'd put it like that. She'd been around Bruno too much. "They hope to God she'll come out of it," her mother said.

"They don't know," Elena said bitterly. "*Doctors.*"

"I don't believe that perfume, though," Nina said. "And expensive. How could you spend so much on perfume?"

"Ma," Joanie said.

"Hey, you ever see her?" Sandro said. He gave up and got back in his chair. He was trying to get the lacrosse helmet off. "The least she could do is smell good."

Nina took the pan with the sausage and peppers out of the broiler and dropped it on the floor. Everybody jumped. The peppers spattered over a big area and just missed Sandro's leg.

"Ho. *Ho,*" Sandro said. Everyone else made exclamations.

Someone banged on the screen door. Elena always locked it when she visited: her cousin's sister on Stratford Avenue, one day they walked right in.

"What's the deal with the security?" Bruno said from outside. "The Mucherinos sense trouble? Gangland *hit?*"

"You're not gettin' in without a present," Sandro said. He was lifting his feet so Nina could clean under the table. Joanie got a sponge and some paper towels and helped out.

"Open the goddamn *door* I'm not gettin' in without a present," Bruno said.

Elena got up from her chair and fumbled with the lock. Neither she nor Bruno said anything while she worked on it. At one point something clicked and she thought she had it. Bruno rattled the handle.

Elena opened the door and stood back.

"Mrs. DeFeo," he said, exasperated. He was still standing outside, and she was still holding the door. "Good to *see* you."

"Bruno," Elena said. She thought Bruno was hardworking but a pig. He shit on my Nancy, she had told Nina and Joanie.

"Look at *this,* look at this," Bruno said, coming

in. "Howdy howdy howdy howdy howdy. Todd's party. The party for Todd."

"J'ou bring a gift?" Sandro said. He still had his feet up in the air while Nina cleaned, and he looked like he was on a ride. Joanie told him to put his feet down.

Nina finished. Joanie could see how upset she was: mice in the kitchen, no food, the kid's father not even here, nothing going right. At the sink, rinsing out the sponge, Joanie said, "Ma, don't worry," meaning the spill.

"Did I bring a *gift?*" Bruno said. "Is it out there on the step right now?"

He looked at Todd. Todd shrugged, as if to say, I don't know.

"Did I bring a gift?" Bruno said, opening the screen door again. Elena was still standing beside him, waiting for him to settle somewhere before she sat down. "In terms of gifts, I think it's time to visit Mr. Excess," he said. He bent down for something right outside the door.

He brought in a square box. It was wrapped in newspaper. Joanie had a frightened flash that it was another lacrosse helmet, that everybody knew about Todd and lacrosse but her.

Bruno caught her looking at him. She thought,

34

This guy. Why's he so interested? Why's he so hot for *me?*

She inventoried him. He was no kid. He was no Mr. *GQ*, though he usually dressed better than the other guys at Goewey Buick, that was for sure. He had baby skin, but the kind of show-through beard where you had to shave five times a day. No gray. Nice mouth, but his face was jowly. Nice shoes always, Italian, very thin leather. When he stood around like now, he kept raising and lowering his toes, a little gesture of impatience you could watch for.

She looked away and there was Nancy, taking in everything, as usual.

"The kid is a football fan, the kid is a Viking fan," Bruno said while Todd unwrapped the thing. "Did I buy him a shirt? Did I buy him a *pennant?*"

Todd pulled the box free of the paper. It was a football helmet, a Minnesota Vikings football helmet.

"God," he said. "It's great."

"Real thing," Bruno said. "The one they wear."

"Where'd you get that?" Sandro said.

"Where'd I get it? I stole it from the locker room. I own the team," Bruno said. "Where'd I get it."

"This must be helmet night," Elena said.

Bruno turned around and gave her a look. "They

sell 'em in sporting goods stores," he said. "You should see. It's a sight to behold."

"Bruno, that's too much," Joanie said. "That musta cost a lot."

"You're *welcome,*" Bruno said. Joanie's great-aunt Clorinda was peering at him. He waved at her. "Bruno, have a seat," he said. "Bruno, have some wine."

"Bruno, have a seat," Sandro said. "Have some wine."

Elena's chair was next to Nancy's. Bruno sat in it like he'd paid for it. "How are *you,* Nancy?" he said.

"Bruno, I'm fine," Nancy said.

"That's good," Bruno said.

Sandro got up to get another chair. He told Elena to sit in his.

He flipped the record while he was up. Because of the awkwardness of Bruno and Nancy together, everyone listened. Lou Monte again: "Please, Mr. Columbus, Turn-a the Ship Around."

"Lou Monte," Bruno said when Sandro came back into the kitchen toting a chair. "Very, very classy. I myself prefer Topo Gigio."

"Mr. Sophisticated," Sandro said. He got Bruno a glass.

"I still need to have Wayne Newton explained to

me, too," Bruno said. He turned the glass upside down and cleaned it with his napkin. "Anybody have any ideas, please get right on it. I'm listening."

"Oh, I like him," Elena said, from over by the door.

Nancy sang the chorus of "Danke Schoen."

"We got a mouse over here," Sandro said. "You missed the big hunt."

"A mouse," Bruno said. "You oughta get Sewer Mouth over here." Because Audrey slobbered on him, he called her Sewer Mouth.

"Bruno, that was too much," Joanie said. She pointed at the helmet. Todd now had both helmets bumping and clacking together on his lap.

"It cost a bundle," Bruno said. "You guys are forever in my *debt*."

He turned to the great-aunt. "How we doin', Clorinda?" he said in his louder-for-the-folks-in-the-Home voice. "You gettin' out?"

"Hah?" Clorinda said.

"Leave her alone," Nancy said, but she seemed to be enjoying it.

"I said, You gettin' out? Dance?" He danced a little figure across the table with his first two fingers.

"Ha," Clorinda said.

"Nina, siddown," Sandro said. "The antipasto's enough."

Everyone agreed. She brought over the remaining sausage and peppers, with some garlic bread in a smaller dish. She seemed to feel better once she had them on the table.

"How's business, Bruno?" Sandro said. He liked to bait him, for laughs.

"Don't talk to me about business," Bruno said, pouring wine.

Sandro said he looked like he was doing good. Todd yawned widely. It was pretty late for him already, Joanie thought.

Hey, do I look at your bankbook?" Bruno said. "What're you, the IRS?"

"I thought maybe you could lend me some money," Sandro said. He winked at Joanie.

"I'll lend you this," Bruno said. His hand was between his legs.

"Bruno," Nina said.

He folded his hands in prayer before him and shook them to show what he had to put up with. "Hey, I'm sorry. Today I had the three lonely guys. The last guy, he wanted to be my friend. He wanted to be with me forever. The guy wants to talk, he wants to relate, he wants to go for long walks in the moonlight, he wants to do everything but buy the fucking car. Pardon my French."

He caught Joanie's eyes before she could throw

Nancy a sympathetic look. He always, always antic-
ipated her. Two days after Gary left, she'd suddenly
been bedridden at her parents': couldn't eat a thing,
threw up night and day, sweated like a horse. Bruno
called the house. "How's Joanie?" he asked. "She sick
yet?"

Nancy passed him the garlic bread, and he took
it without looking at it. "This guy, I led him all
around the lot, we come into my office to talk numbers. He sits down, he goes, *'Field of Dreams*. There's
a great movie.' I thought, Give me one break. Not
this. Not now. *Field of Dreams*. Dead baseball players
hang out in the tall corn. Every so often, bip, there
they are again. Back in the tall corn, huh? I'll tell you
what: a guy comes in and tells me he likes that kind
of movie, he might as well just spread the inside of
his wallet out on my desk. Just spread it all out and
say, 'Take what you want and leave me bus fare.' "

"I *liked Field of Dreams*," Sandro said. "Wasn't
that the one with Robert Redford?"

"You don't know," Bruno said. "Last movie you
saw was *Pride of the Yankees*."

They got down to serious eating. The sausages
went around the table. People split them so there'd
be enough. Bruno got up to go to the bathroom, and
when he squeezed by Joanie on the way back, he
trailed his fingertips across her shoulder. He was

39

looking at her when he sat down. She raised her chin, worried she looked as ragged and uncomposed as a kid who ran away from home.

"I like your hair like that, Mrs. Muhlberg," he said. She had it up, because of the heat.

"Bruno, you're something," Nina said, eating.

"I like her *hair,*" he said. He turned his palms up.

Joanie thought, At least I'm generating interest from somebody. She also liked the minor rebelliousness of the public flirting.

Before Gary took off, she'd been with Bruno at the funeral of one of Bruno's friends, Mark Siegler. At the cemetery, they'd ended up on opposite sides of the grave. He'd made faces. She'd shot him a look, and he'd pointed to his crotch and arched his eyebrows.

"Someone called for you," Joanie said. "Before."

Bruno was instantly alert. "Oh yeah?" he said. "Who?"

She shrugged. "He didn't sound happy. He said he'd see you later tonight," she said.

Bruno looked at her. He flexed his shoulders to fix his shirt. He nodded.

They ran out of wine. Sandro stood up to get more.

"Sandro, get Joey's homemade," Nina said. "The one Bruno brought last time."

"Which one's Joey's?" Sandro said.

"Look, there are two reds down there right next to each other," Nina said. She held up two fingers, like a peace sign. "Get *this* one, not *this* one." She tilted her hand to favor each finger.

Everybody laughed. Joanie looked cross-eyed at Todd. It was a thing they exchanged whenever anyone said something stupid. Sandro put his hand over his eyes.

"That's a help, Nin," Sandro said. "I'll get this one." He put his finger in his nose. He squeezed by Joanie, and they heard him going down the cellar stairs.

"So Todd's a grown-up now," Bruno said. His joking had changed. He looked preoccupied. Joanie filed the information: a Bruno weak spot, something to do with the call.

"Man o' the house," Bruno said.

Todd shrugged.

"I missed the ceremony," Bruno said.

"Dere're *tree* bottles down here," Sandro called from the cellar.

"Get this one," Bruno called back without raising his head, holding up his middle finger.

Joanie got up to go to the bathroom herself, laughing. The phone rang when she passed it, like she'd tripped an alarm.

She'd forgotten her husband. Todd was upright, alert again. She put her hand on the phone.

She answered it in front of everyone in the kitchen, turning so they could get maximum coverage. She said hello.

"Hello? Joanie?" Gary said. There was a sheeting noise behind him. She imagined a booth on an Arctic traffic median, the Alaska pipeline running alongside. Snow. But it was summer in Alaska, too. "Joanie?" Gary said.

"No," Joanie said. "This's Beatrice." The line was quiet and she knew he was working on that: was he being played with? Meanwhile she enjoyed the reactions from the kitchen.

He introduced himself. He asked for Todd. Joanie told him to hold on and she passed the phone across the table to her son.

"Hey, Dad," Todd said. He had the phone in both hands. "Yeah, she's crazy."

"You're crazy," Nina said to her. Joanie made a face.

She sat back down and took some provolone and bread on her plate, unable to go to the bathroom now without looking like she wanted to be out of the room.

Todd went over what he got. And the jacket,

Joanie thought. "Oh, and Mom got me a jacket," he said.

People kept their voices down. Clorinda sat beside Todd with a stiff silence, cutting her *capacolla* with a knife and fork. Elena murmured to Sandro. Nina looked at the receiver like her grandson was talking to Lee Harvey Oswald. Joanie could see how much it bothered her that the mess had already gotten this normalized. Everyone got away with everything except her family, and this was another example.

The mouse, she noticed, was on the windowsill.

Bruno saw it. He touched Sandro's arm. It was crouching behind a cactus in a green plastic pot. Its back was bent. It apparently hoped it was hidden.

Todd was still talking to his dad. Sandro got up, nonchalant, to get a drink of water from the sink. He swung a hand at the mouse, a little swing, and it bolted across the counter, across the stove. Its paws made tinny scrabbling sounds on the stove top.

Sandro banged a hand after it and just missed. All four coils jumped. The mouse threw itself from the counter, little legs splaying in the air. It landed audibly in front of Joanie and reversed direction back past Bruno. He brought one big shoe down—*boom*—and all the noise stopped. The floor was still reverberating.

Joanie was afraid to look. Bruno looked at each

of them and then down at his foot. He lifted his shoe, slowly, and on the linoleum there was a little curl of a tip of tail, like a gray fingernail.

"Dad, you should call back," Todd said. But the party broke up before he did.

Everyone thanked Nina for having them, and Nina thanked everyone for coming. Joanie and Todd and Bruno helped with the cleanup.

At the screen door with her mother, Nancy said, "You sticking around, Bruno?" and Bruno said yeah, he was sticking around. Nancy left.

"Mrs. Mucherino does not like Mr. Mouse," Bruno said when Nina came back to the sink.

"I'm not too fond of Mr. Minea, either," Nina said, taking the dish towel from him.

"It's all right, I failed," Bruno said. "I had him right in my sights—*budaboom*—I didn't finish it. I have to live with that."

Sandro told him to give the mouse a rest.

When they were finished, they went out in the driveway and stood around Joanie's Buick. It was warm and the crickets were loud. Todd loaded his presents in the back. The phone started ringing, but Todd didn't hear it and no one else brought it up.

"How's the car running?" Bruno asked. It was a ritual question, a "do I look out for you or do I look out for you?" question. He'd sold it to them. It was a dark-blue Century wagon. It looked like a hearse. It had an expanse of hood she never really got used to. He gave it to them cheap when it was three years old and had twenty thousand miles on it. Now it had a hundred and the body was dinged up, but it ran, no problem. When her father talked about it, he said, "That automobile doesn't owe you a penny." He pronounced it auto*m*obile.

Gary had taken the Mazda with him, so the Buick was it as far as transportation went.

Joanie told him the car ran great.

"That automobile doesn't owe her a penny," Sandro said.

"That car was some deal," Bruno said. He was looking around and down the street, like he was expecting company.

"I know it," Joanie said.

"So, you gonna go home, or what?" Bruno said. "You tired?" She could see faint hopes fading. "You're probably tired."

"Todd's pretty worn out," she said.

"Thanks a lot for the helmet," Todd said. He'd said good-bye to Nina and Sandro and was already in the car.

Nina came and gave her a hug. "I'm sorry about the way things turned out," she said bitterly.

Joanie told her not to worry and said good-bye.

That seemed to make things worse. Sandro followed
his wife into the house with a look back at Joanie that
said, Thanks a lot.

They heard banging around, the raspy sound of
foil torn from the roll. The crickets started up. Todd
was slumped against the headrest and looked already
asleep.

They stood next to the car for a minute, awkward.

"What was the deal with that call?" Joanie said.

Bruno shrugged.

"Looked like it upset you," she said.

He snorted.

She thought, I don't need this. She hoped something would happen.

He took her cheek with his fingertips and turned
her head and kissed her. She felt a rush of caffeine.
She felt her lips after his were gone.

"Bruno, don't start," she said.

He was looking at her. "Hey, when I start, you'll
know it," he said. He looked in on Todd, who hadn't
moved. He cupped his hand around the back of her
neck. He left.

She got in the car and started it. She turned on
the headlights. The objects down the driveway were
flooded with illumination. They promised her something. In the rearview mirror, Bruno's taillights

winked red at the end of the street and disappeared. She left the radio alone. She had, while she sat there, what she thought of as a little religious spasm, like she'd been confronted by objects ready to help her take part in the transformation of her world.

Todd revived on the way home. Joanie was speeding. She was charged up. She didn't know why. He shifted around on his seat and retied his sneakers.

She was heading up 110 to the Merritt Parkway. One-ten ran along the river, with a state park on the other side. It felt like the country. The road was twisty and had no streetlights and she liked it; it never had cops on it this time of night, and she knew it well enough to go fast. Her high beams were on. Even the Buick was leaning on the curves. Presents slid across the backseat.

When she drove, she set speed contests for herself: Could she make this part of the trip in under ten minutes? Could she make all three of these lights? It was a way of getting from place to place. Her driving had gotten better since Gary left. Todd had taken to riding with his feet up on the dash, bracing himself.

They jounced along, swooping across curves and lanes. They flashed past something small and dead, with a little foot in the air, near a storm drain. Possum? Raccoon? She caught only a glimpse of it. Todd sighed. She considered various questions—Did you have a good time? Like your presents? What'd your father say?—but didn't ask any of them.

"I wonder if Audrey came back," he said.

"I'm sure she did," Joanie said.

"This's the longest she stayed away," he said.

She didn't have anything to say to that, so she kept quiet.

He sat up straight and turned to the backseat and rooted around in his presents. "Looking for your jacket?" she asked ironically.

He pulled out Nancy's book. He was peering at it in the dark.

She turned on the overhead light. She steadied the wheel. "Read me something," she said.

"Play the radio," Todd said.

"C'mon. Read me something," she said.

"Ma."

"What is it, just a collection of stories?"

"It's all different tales."

"What're they called? Give me some titles," she said. They went over a bump and the car almost bottomed out. She overcorrected for a curve. Todd gave her a look.

He flipped around and found the contents page. " 'The Man Wreathed in Seaweed,' " he read. " 'The Man Who Came Out Only at Night.' 'Body–without–Soul.' 'The Little Girl Sold with the Pears.' "

"Read me that one," she said.

"*Ma*," he said.

"Just a *lit*tle."

He sighed. He rubbed his nose industriously and scratched so she could hear it. He sighed again. " 'Once a man had a pear tree that used to bear four baskets of pears a year. One year, though, it only bore three baskets and a half, while he was supposed to carry four to the king. Seeing no other way out, he put his youngest daughter into the fourth basket and covered her up with pears and leaves.' "

They passed a pull-off with some parked cars. Teenagers, Joanie thought.

"Yeah?" she said. Her eyes were on the yellow lines ribboning out and dipping and reappearing in the distance. "Go on."

"We shouldn't drive with the light on like this," Todd said.

Joanie made a face at the road ahead and snapped off the overhead light. They were quiet for a few miles.

As usual, what she wanted to say would make her sound like someone she didn't want to sound like. So she kept her mouth shut. This was the way she usually felt when he was acting up: reasonable and trampled.

She turned on the radio and cranked it. "Everybody awake, pal, let's go," she said. She felt reckless, the irresponsible mother.

It was a "classic rock" station. They were halfway through The Who's "Won't Get Fooled Again." Roger Daltrey screamed.

It charged her up further. She'd been a big Who fan.

"Aw, jeez," Todd said, sinking in his seat.

Lately, up-tempo rock acted on her accelerator, she noticed. "Won't Get Fooled Again" segued into The Yardbirds' "Train Kept a-Rollin'," another all-time favorite. She touched the dial out of reflex, in appreciation, but didn't take the volume any higher. The rhythm line galloped her into the song.

She could see the bridge up ahead and the entrance to the parkway, black water, power lines, little yellow lights doubled off docks on the Milford side.

A man, a face showing teeth, was there in front of her and took her breath. Wide eyes, a black jacket. She felt an electric spasm of shock. Todd screamed.

The body seemed to hurl itself out, lunged at her

and thudded. The bumper turned him, and he cart-wheeled and hit the roof of the car. She felt the sound in her heart. She heard him carried down the length of the roof, like someone running in heavy boots, and then he was off. Their car careened right and then left and skidded into bushes that splintered and snapped along one side, like gunfire. Todd was bounced into her and she was slung across Todd. The hood flew up. They stopped.

She was aware that the noise of their shrieks and the braking had died away. The Yardbirds were louder, and into the next chorus. She turned the radio off. There was a whimpering, like someone else was in the car. She turned the engine off, but it continued, shaking and then ticking.

"Ma, what'd we do?" Todd whispered. She could see his eyes in the darkness. She checked to see if he was all right. She checked to see if she was. They both shook. The car's ticking wound down.

She tried to get the courage to open her door. She looked back. The body was off the side of the road. One leg was crossed over the other, like someone had flopped down for a nap near the white line.

She had to get out. Someone else could come along. The guy could still be alive. She had to help. She had the feeling her life was a movie that just tore—a whole set of concerns, a world, cut away and flapping. She was looking at the whiteness of the screen.

She had to get up. She had to function. She held the wheel and could feel herself trying to shudder the fear out. It worked a little. She opened the door. Her movements occurred without her full cooperation.

She crossed the pavement to the body. "Stay there," she called hoarsely back to the car. Todd hadn't moved.

They'd skidded a hundred feet past it. She could see the long helixes of skid marks. She got closer and stopped ten feet or so away. This was cowardice, she knew. She willed him up. If she gave him another second, he'd stir, shake his head like someone surfacing from a dive in the pool. He'd turn to her with a look that would let her know he appreciated what a tight squeak *that'd* been.

There was a finger-sized area of blood, discreet, near his head.

This broke her paralysis. She crossed to him and crouched.

He was facedown. A hand and at least a leg were broken; she could see that much already. She didn't want to turn him over. She placed a palm on his back. This seemed to her the best moment for the miracle.

"Is he all right?" Todd called from the car in a small, terrified voice.

"I don't know yet," she said. She moved her hand from the back and put it along the side of the neck, below an ear. She didn't know how to tell if someone was alive. She didn't feel anything. She couldn't hear anything. He didn't look that hurt, but there was the blood from his head. It was very dark. She couldn't see where the blood was coming from.

She leaned back in her crouch, her forehead cooling in panic. She shouldn't move him, but she shouldn't leave him here. The car: she'd have to bring the car around, block the road, put her emergency blinkers on.

She looked closer at his head and neck. It welled up inside her like a confirmation of her worst sense of herself: he was dead. There was more blood, under his chest. She could see the edge of the jacket soaking it up like a spill.

Something cracked in the forest off the side of the road. She got up and walked fast, the little girl turning her back to the haunted house, walked back to the car. Todd was crouched inside, his head low and his knees up. One of the presents, the board game, had flown onto his lap. He clawed it away from him with some alarm.

She moved along the front of the car. The hood was sprung, but otherwise looked no worse than it usually did. She shut it and it stayed down. The bumper had a gentle dent under the right headlight. It did not stand out. The body was pushed in a little, too. She imagined people in the woods. She got in the car. She started it. She was in a new world.

She edged the gas, and they pulled free of the bushes with a bump and rocked onto the road. Leaves were caught under the windshield wipers. She turned right. She was thinking, I can go for help instead of waiting here. She was thinking the first gas station or cop car. Todd didn't say anything.

Something scraped and dragged beneath the car and then fell away. In slow motion, she pulled onto the ramp for the Merritt Parkway. She thumped up onto the shoulder and straightened the car out.

Todd shifted around in his seat. He peered over the side of his door. "Where're we going?" he asked.

Where were they going? "We're gonna call," she said. She didn't know where.

They were going too slow. They were crossing the bridge. She could hear the whine of the bridge metal beneath them. A car rushed by her, swerved, and honked. She turned on her lights.

"That was a phone booth down there," Todd said, meaning farther along 110. "There's no phone booths up here."

"We could call from home," she said, and knew

it was wrong when she said it. She looked over at Todd. He was looking at her piercingly.

Was she crazy? This was possible. She saw exit signs ahead. She slowed down and took the exit.

"Now where're we going?" Todd said. "What're you *do*ing?" He sounded a little hysterical.

At the stop sign, she looked both ways. She turned left. She turtled forward under the highway, and stopped, and looked both ways again. The road, whatever it was, was dark and quiet. She turned left again.

"I'm going back," she said.

He didn't say anything.

Heading back toward the body, she thought of her life changed: she saw newspapers, flashbulbs, and jury trials, all images from movies. The triviality and theatricality of her imagination were appalling. You killed someone, she thought. But even that was theatrical and lacked weight, as if she were a scold.

The tires drummed back onto the bridge. A police car appeared from behind them and surged by, and its siren bolted on as it passed. As she came over the crest of the arc she saw the lights, yellow and blue, flashing around the scene of the accident. There were red taillights glowing, too: two or three cars. Her heart seized up. The police car that had passed her slowed as much as it could and careened off onto 110. She sailed frozenly by the exit.

"What're we doin'?" Todd cried. "What're you *do*in'?"

"*Shut up,*" she said, and he gave off a wail, and put his head in his hands, and left it at that.

God forgive me, God forgive me, she said to herself.

That meant she had to turn around again and go back. The car handled like a truck. The wheel lurched and jerked at her hands. Once again: under the highway, up the entrance ramp. It was nightmarish. She was becoming something comic. They could see the scene yet again. Various people were illuminated in red, posed kneeling and crouching around the central figure of the body. It reminded her of a Christmas crèche, and she was amazed at her blasphemy and detachment. She couldn't conceive of herself as part of that group now: driving up, approaching the cops standing around their cars, and saying, I did this.

They were back on the bridge. Todd looked out the window at the river, his head against the headrest in despair.

You can call from home, she thought. She had to go back, she understood. But leaving had made it impossible to return: she was twice as criminal. Three times as criminal.

"I'm trying to think," she said. Todd didn't answer.

The car was making ominous, rhythmic scraping noises, and she thought, not even sure what she meant, Not this, too.

She passed the exit where she'd turned around the first time. She had the feeling she was coming to moral turning points, one after the other, and failing each one. She kept putting a hand to her cheek, as if to cool it.

When she slowed for their exit, Todd said, "It's hit-and-run. It's hit-and-run if you leave him and don't say anything."

Joanie took an audibly deep breath and let it out, as if she were blowing smoke. She recognized it as what she did to signal Todd during debates that things were a lot more complicated in the adult world than he realized; that sometimes she wished he only knew how patient she could be. She let the fraudulence of her response stand. Todd didn't seem much affected by it, anyway.

"If you leave him—" Todd said.

"I *know*," she said, trying to control her voice. She swung into a turn so that he slid into the door on his side. "I *know* all of this," she said.

From that point to the turn into their street, she ran through variations on Why me? and Why does this have to happen now?

The garage door was open, though the light was out. She sailed right up the driveway and braked only at the last minute. Lucky he had put his bike away this time, she thought grimly. The front bumper clanked the junk against the wall. She turned the engine off and hung forward on the wheel.

Nested bicycle fenders and a hubcab Gary'd hung on a nail were still making noise. The streetlight penetrated only as far as the back bumper, so she could just about see her hands.

"You were going too fast," Todd said.

"Was it my fault?" Joanie said. "Did he just come out of nowhere at us, or not?"

"You were going too fast," Todd said.

"I was *not* going too fast," Joanie said. "I was not going that fast."

Todd shifted around on the seat next to her. It was possible he'd refuse to get out of the car. Decide to go next door and call the police.

"How could I have seen him in time?" she said. "What could anybody have done?"

Her ears were ringing, like she'd been shouting. She sat back against the seat and closed her eyes. She'd been going too fast.

The engine was ticking as it cooled, the way it did after the accident. Todd noticed it, too, and got out of the car and slammed the door. When she got to the front door, he was standing there with his head down, like a dog waiting to be let in.

"I'm going to call," she said as she wrestled with the key. She swung the door inward, and he slipped by her and through the front hall.

"How 'bout some lights?" she said. He went directly to the back door.

She hit the lights and put her bag down and stood near the phone. Her chest felt the way she did at the beach when she'd breathed in too much water, too much mist.

"Audrey's back," Todd said. He opened the door, and the dog pitter-pattered in across the tile.

He closed it behind her and relocked it and crossed to the kitchen table. He sat in one of the chairs. Audrey checked her dish and then walked over to him and put her head beside his knee. He played with her ears. He was waiting for Joanie to call.

She had her hand on the phone. It was a wall phone, white. It reminded her of hours ago at her mother's. She let it go and pulled open the junk drawer beneath it. She pulled out the phone book and searched the municipal section at the front. Pages slapped back and forth.

"You could just dial nine-one-one," Todd said.

She ignored him.

She found the precinct number and dialed. Todd was looking at the dog. She had her hand on the phone, for support. It was ringing at the other end. Her index finger swung over into the cradle and pressed the switch hook. She took her hand away before he could see. Look what you're doing, she thought, as horrified as she'd been at any other point that night. She pressed the earpiece tighter to her head. He'd hear the dial tone, she thought.

"Hello," she said. "I'd like to report— Yes," she said. "Yes." She stopped. The dial tone was deafening. She thought of the story she'd read in junior high, the murdered man's heart you could hear under the floor.

She covered the mouthpiece with her hand. "They got me on hold," she said.

Todd was still contemplating Audrey, testing the floppiness of her ears.

Minutes went by. Joanie didn't know what to do. Her mashed ear was sore. She wanted Todd to leave, to take some pressure off the second part of her performance.

"Get ready for bed," she said. "I'll be right up."

He looked up at her with surprise, and she had the terrified premonition she'd blown it. "They're gonna want to interview us and stuff," he said. "I can't go to bed."

"They're gonna want to interview *me,*" she said. "They're not gonna want to interview you. Why would they want to interview you?"

"I'm going with you," he said stubbornly. "They'd want to interview me."

She felt a rush of shame, his loyalty juxtaposed to her weakness, her ongoing lying.

She was still standing there with the phone.

"Try nine-one-one," he said.

She hung up.

"I'll call them tomorrow," she said, but his face when she said that made her turn back to the phone, and, exasperated, as if he'd been relentlessly asking they stop for ice cream, she dialed 911. What she'd do now she didn't know. Try the hang-up thing again?

When the busy signal came on, she angrily held the receiver out for Todd to hear.

When she hung up again, he started to cry. She crossed the kitchen and knelt beside him and hugged him. She was crying, too. The dog walked around them in circles.

She checked him again to make sure he was okay. She took him upstairs. He got undressed and into bed. She went into the bathroom and leaned on the sink, her arms spread apart and holding her weight. She used the Pond's to take off what little eye makeup she had on and washed her face.

It was hot but breezy. Her bedroom windows were open. She maneuvered around her room in the dark and got on the bed, still in her clothes, and lay on her back. Downstairs, the dog was making the rounds, her license tag clinking on the metal water dish. Todd was crying quietly in his room.

She slapped at herself, spread her fingers over her face and pulled at it. She had to talk to people, her father maybe. She thought of Bruno, what he would say.

What frightened her most was her inability to picture the terrible things ahead. It seemed like the best evidence of how inadequate she was.

She imagined a generalized scandal, everyone's understanding of her changed. Maybe Todd taken away from her.

You *killed* somebody, she thought. Someone's dead because of you, and this is what you think about, this is what you're worried about.

He could've had a family, she thought.

What was he doing in the *road?* What was he doing there in the road?

At some point she heard Todd get up, the bedsprings, the floorboards. He was going downstairs.

She got up, too, still dressed. It was late. She was chilly and walked with her arms folded.

She found him in the kitchen. He was eating M&M's in the dark. He'd put them in a little bowl. The bowl caused her a pang: he always got neat when he was scared.

She was going to pull a chair over next to his but suddenly was too tired even for that. She sat on the floor beside him, her head on his thigh. He didn't say anything.

She half dozed. She had the impression he was alert, awake, the whole time. The kitchen floor, the walls, were getting lighter. Through the doorway to the living room, she could make out shapes of chairs and a small table. Did she own these things? She remembered Todd that morning at breakfast, smiling speechlessly. She remembered nodding to herself as she drove, as if consenting to her life.

"We're not going to tell anyone, are we, Mom?" he said above her. His voice was so pitiful and despairing that it hurt too much to answer him. The M&M's rolled and clicked together in the bowl like abacus beads. He put his hand on her head, tentatively. He came down to the floor with her and brought the bowl.

Outside, some garbage cans clanked. On the floor, his legs stuck straight out and his shoes were run over at the heels.

He finally fell asleep. His mouth was open against her shoulder. She listened to morning birds with cries like the workings of scissors. She sat there with her son and waited for the next thing.

BRUNO

I WAS GOING to give Joanie a ride to her mother's for her kid's confirmation party, I couldn't, I had to show this Korean every single fucking thing about a Dodge Dart we had on the lot, a trade-in from 1901. He wants to see all the paperwork, he wants to climb underneath it, he wants to go through the buyer's manual like he's prepping for a space shot. The manual's so old it's coming apart in our hands. It's six-forty-five and he's not buying today, we can see that, but he's not going anywhere, either.

This is a Buick dealership. I'm wearing a Buick pin. We're surrounded by Buicks. Showroom floor is wall to wall with them. The guy goes, Do you sell Buicks here? I go, No, we give 'em away. That's how we stay in business: giving away free Buicks.

This guy couldn't decide on a shitbox Dodge

Dart, there's no chance in the *world* he's going to spring for a full-ticket Buick.

He goes, Are they dependable cars?

I go, Look, Boulder Dam shut down a few times last year. You want me to guarantee a lousy six-thousand-dollar car?

He's taking all this in, giving it some hard thought. The minute hand's going around. He wants to know, Do they come with automatic transmission and air at no extra charge? I tell him, You bet they do. Not only that, but we throw in a free dinner and tickets to a Broadway show. What's he think we're running here, a raffle?

We're standing around talking afterwards in the office, and Cifulo's giving me this look, and I'm watching the clock while this guy sips his coffee and stares into space. The missus is sitting there with him and clearly has veto power but doesn't say boo. I'm making conversation, so I ask him if he's Japanese. Big mistake: turns out he's Korean. The missus is miffed.

Afterward Cifulo gives me grief about it, so I tell him, What, that's better? Far as I'm concerned, they're boat people with an attitude. They got here earlier, they're better? I say no. They run dink grocery stores, three dollars for a banana. There's one guy on

Barnum Avenue, I still don't know his name. SHIMSI, the sign says. What is that? Two names? His name? BUY OUR FOOD? One thing's for sure: you want to get some service, don't ask Kato behind the counter.

Cifulo tells me afterward I was rude to them. This imbecile moving two units a month, if he's lucky and his family comes in, is telling *me* how to run my business. I told him, What are you talking to me for? You watch Steven Seagal movies. *Out for Violence, Revenge Is Mine*—whatever they're called. I told him, Steven Seag*al?* The man wears a ponytail? Is this the *Revolution?* And Sea-*gal:* what is that? The guy's not a Jew anymore? And what are you, what are you, Bishop Sheehan? Mother Teresa?

So it turns out I couldn't give Joanie this ride.

They talk about ups and downs in the car business, but we been down a while. I'm always high man for monthly sales, but what is that? Every day we stand around the showroom like CYO kids waiting for the party to begin.

Now on toppa that I gotta worry about this Monteleone thing.

Things are gonna go wrong. It's not like things are always gonna go right. The key is how we deal with it. How do we act? I say, I can't control everything. But I have to deal with it.

Joanie, for example. I coulda pushed it the other night, after that kiss. I wanted to push it. But it's not right.

You got to have a little class, a little understanding of the way to do things. In Italy, the old gentlemen, they cultivate *tratto,* you know, a *elegance,* a way you handle yourself, conduct your affairs.

She's coming around. She doesn't know it, her mother doesn't know it, nobody probably knows it. But she's coming around.

There will be setbacks. I understand that. Remember: if it isn't one thing, it will surely be another. What's important? Your attitude.

NINA

THE CHURCH was very big for my mother. She came over when she must've been thirty-one, thirty-two, four kids in tow and one on the way. I think the Church was a big help. It was a place she could trust, she had the priest she could talk to. Plus it was a big connection to Strangolagalli, to what she knew. Right before we came over, one of my little brothers died; he was just a baby. Our priest there, Father Picarazzi, was a big help. She was still sad when she got here, so naturally she went to the priest here, too.

She prayed a lot at home, usually early early in the morning, before we all were up. She had all the little statues in her bedroom. And the pictures with the palms still behind them from whenever the last Palm Sunday was.

Our church was St. Anthony's on North Avenue. Not St. Anthony of Padua, who helped people find lost things—the other St. Anthony. The one in the desert who was always resisting the temptations of the devil. The devil showed up at his hut in the form of a pig. Just what the temptation was involving the pig, we didn't know. Maybe the devil was tempting him with bacon. But how big a temptation was that? It seemed like a lot of work. He had to kill the pig, etc. Anyway, the pig was in the stained-glass windows above the confessionals on the right side of the church. I prayed on that side. I was a little girl, twelve years old, just about Todd's age. It sounds terrible now, but I used to pray sometimes to the pig. He was small and they did him cute. I guess I didn't believe it was really the devil. I think I figured everybody pictured in church had to be good.

The confessionals on the other side didn't get any light. They were much darker. They were used by visiting priests. You'd go in there, it'd be like a cave. You couldn't see the priest and you didn't know him anyway. So you went there if you had serious sins to confess or you hadn't been to confession in a long time. It was good for gossip: we'd watch who went over there. Oh, Mr. Motz: what's *he* doing over there? So it kind of backfired on you.

It was a very Italian church. Father Favale was the priest for thirty, thirty-five years. He joked every

Pentecost Sunday that our sins were committed in Italian, confessed in English, and pardoned in Latin.

There was one sister always used to joke with me that because of me she prayed to St. Jude, patron saint of lost causes. She thought I was a hopeless case because I wasn't religious enough.

She'd make notes when I was bad, like in the middle of the winter, and she wouldn't punish me then. When it was spring and beautiful out, then she'd keep me after school. I could hear all the kids running around and having a great time, and she'd say, Nina, remember when you did this? And when you did that?

But I was good kid for the most part.

My mother was worried about my lying. I lied, you know, like kids do. I wasn't a big liar. My mother believed as long as you never told a lie you were always on God's side. The most important thing was to tell the truth. You did something wrong, okay. But it was worse to lie about it. And if you lied, that was bad enough. It was worse to pretend that you hadn't lied, and to keep going: every second you lived the lie was another sin.

They'd hit us when we got caught. But not so often; it wasn't like other schools. It was funny: when you were getting hit, you thought the world was like that. Then afterwards when you met other people who weren't Catholic or didn't get hit in school, you thought: it *isn't* like that. And then, sometime after that, you realized the world *was* like that, after all. So then you thought maybe you were better off knowing early.

TODD

THE WORST THING up to now I ever did was commit a sacrilege. The way we were taught, a sacrilege was this huge thing, and really rare. It didn't seem so rare to us. The sisters made it a big thing and then they didn't. You couldn't tell. For instance, in fifth grade these two guys got into a fight. Sister Amalia tried to break it up and got punched in the chest. She was upset. She sat there on the floor holding herself and said it was a sacrilege. The kid who did it was scared. But we didn't believe her. We didn't think she was that holy. Also, it was an accident, and we didn't think you could get a sacrilege that way. We made the kid feel better. Later he was coming back from Communion at Easter and he held up his arm for us, right there in church. The sisters didn't know what he meant, but we did: he was going, Here's my arm; it hasn't fallen off yet.

But there was another kind that wasn't accidental. One year our parish priest went away and the guy who replaced him was mean. In confession he'd go, "C'mon, c'mon," if you stopped to think. And if you said something he didn't like, he'd say, "You did *what?*" You heard it all the time. It was embarrassing. Kids would come out of the booth bright red, or crying.

You couldn't predict what would set him off. Once, I told him I stole some books from the local bookstore—nothing big, two little things on dinosaurs I put under my sweater—and it must've been the nineteenth case of that, that day, or he must've just been sick of it or something. He blew up. He said, "*What* did you do that for? What were you *think*ing?" And then he said, "You could afford to buy something like that. Your parents could afford it." So everybody out in church knew I must've stolen something. And I said without thinking, "Don't shout it," and then he got seriously mad. He kept me in there longer than he was supposed to, just yelling at me. He kept his voice down for that. Then he gave me fifty Hail Marys and fifty Our Fathers. Fifty is a huge amount. I had to go to the altar rail and kneel there, and no matter how fast I said them—and after the first ten I was flying—it still looked to everyone in the church like I must've killed my mother.

The worst part was I was so scared of confession after that that I didn't go. I kept not wanting to go to Communion. I had all these mortal sins on my soul. The sisters were like, Why aren't you going to Communion? What could I tell them? So finally I went. The whole way up in the line I was telling myself, *Go back, go back, you're going to commit sacrilege.* Because it's sacrilege to receive with a mortal sin on your soul and you know it.

I stood there in line feeling like such a hypocrite, such a liar, the sisters thinking I was being a good Catholic while I was doing this.

After I received, I went back to my row and put my head on the pew in front of me. I looked up and there was Sister Amalia, and she gave me this smile, like she was happy I was so good. I thought, *You committed a sacrilege just so you wouldn't be embarrassed.*

That night I realized people were going to Hell not only because they were bad but also because they were weak.

I didn't do anything about it for six weeks. Every time I got Communion—because I had to get Communion, otherwise, why wasn't I getting it?—I was committing sacrilege. Sacrilege, sacrilege, sacrilege. All my friends were ahead of me and behind me in line, getting Communion like it was no big deal. Because it wasn't for them. And I kept it all from everyone. Who could I tell? It was like a nightmare; it was so easy to stop, and I wasn't stopping. It was like I thought, What difference did it make? My soul was so black it couldn't get blacker. But it *was* getting blacker. I thought I was setting sacrilege records. I thought somewhere God was thinking that this was all too bad. He knew everything, so he knew I wasn't evil, but that that wasn't going to make things any better. People were going to Hell for stealing a car or for missing Mass. I was going to get off the hook?

Then I found out you *had* to go to confession before confirmation. We went as a group; there was no getting out of it. And I had to confess it, because the bishop would be giving us Communion at the ceremony, and I thought, Even *I* can't do that sacrilege.

So every night the week before, I was up, praying, crying, I didn't know what. I found myself under the bed one night. Finally, the day of the confession, I was the second one in line, the whole class and Sister Amalia out there in the pews, waiting. I was so miserable by then I just gave up. I just went in and said, "Forgive me, Father, for I have sinned. It has been six weeks since my last confession." And he asked why it took me six weeks. I told him because I'd committed this sacrilege. He said, "You did *what?*" I thought, Here we go. But when I explained it, he said, "That's not a sacrilege," like that was obvious. I was so relieved to hear anybody say that that I didn't argue with him. He gave me like fifteen Hail Marys for penance. I was so happy I was all teary-eyed. I still thought it was a sacrilege, but now it was like I had special dispensation; I had a priest tell me not to worry about it.

That was the worst thing I'd done until now.

The other night when I was up with my mother, I remembered all that, remembered being up all night worried about the sacrilege.

This is worse, now, than then. It's like there are two of me wandering around at once. I'm someone else from the person everyone thinks I am.

If I was God, I'd be harder on me than her. She's scared and doesn't believe in everything, anyway. But I learned every day in catechism what the right thing to do was. I was an altar boy. I helped serve Communion. It's like when I had the sacrilege: like every day I'm slapping God in the face, over and over and over.

JOANIE

SERVICES on Good Friday, Stations of the Cross—my mother was one of those Catholics who excused herself from a lot of the duties because she had a hard life. That's what she said. The idea was that God let her off on that.

I think *her* mother always had the harder life. My father's always been good to her, and they've never been poor. Her mother had to come over from Italy with her husband and four kids, start up from nothing. When I remind my mother of that, she says, Yeah, but she didn't have to put up with being me.

By that I think she means that her mother *expected* a lot of unhappiness.

My mother had this thing she would say to herself to cheer herself up: It could always get worse than this. She'd say it in this tough way, like she'd taken somebody's best shot. I remember her saying it once when she'd taken me shopping with her at Read's. I was six years old. I hadn't even known she was unhappy.

She said that to me when Gary left. I said to her, "How could it get worse than this?"—even though even then I could think of ways. She said, "It just could."

Now I say to myself, It could always get worse than this. I repeat it.

My mother's got no patience for unhappiness. She says she has less now even than she used to. Which means she has less patience for anything that might be adding to the problem, like my father or the Church. She was secretary of the Rosary Society for two weeks, they started busting her rocks about the way she wrote up the reports, that was the end of that.

So she joked that God let her off on stuff like that. It was like going to the eleven-o'clock Mass: the really great Catholics, they were there on the dot for the seven-o'clock. My mother and I figured God appreciated that, but he also had the later one for the rest of us. If you spent Saturday night hiding bottles from your husband or bailing your kid out of juvenile detention, or you just felt so bad you wanted to lie there in bed an extra three hours, there was still that last

Mass. It was like Mass for the shirkers and the exhausted.

It wasn't that she didn't believe, even in the Church. She just picked the rules she thought were important, for her sake and ours. Lent she never went for, for example.

She tried to bring me up right. She sent me to Blessed Sacrament. The building was falling apart; the building should have been condemned. There was a hole in the floor of the seventh-grade classroom near the heating vent: the seventh-graders could spit down onto the third-graders.

I had a sister there, Sister St. John of the Cross. I had these Martian cards then, cards about Mars invading the Earth—the whole story took up fifty-something cards. A boy I liked, Lawrence Harrigan, gave me his doubles. I was amazed by them. They had things like frost rays and heat rays: skin coming off the bone while the guy looked down and watched, these Martians grinning. Giant insects that picked guys out of cars. There was one gave me nightmares of a woman with hair like my mother on a web with a huge black-and-red spider. Lawrence said it was like Hell. Lawrence was always looking for ways to bring his problems in line with the Church.

Once a day, I asked Sister St. John of the Cross

if I could go to the lavatory. I moved the time around so it wouldn't look suspicious. I carried the cards in my skirt pocket and spread them out around the toilet in the stall. The third day I did it, wham, the stall door opens, there's Sister St. John.

She said, "I knew you were up to something. I *knew*."

I was trying to get my cards back. I would say anything. I asked her how she knew. She said she could *see* it in my face. She said the guilt was in my face. She said, "I can tell everything you've done." And I knew she could. She'd seen through me. She knew what a horrible girl I was all along, and she'd just let me make things worse, pretending I wasn't, her knowing all the time.

You know the only prayer I ever had that was real, that was from my heart? It was a prayer I said whenever I was really scared: PleaseGod pleaseGod oh pleaseGod, pleaseGod. That was my prayer.

When we were reading about the Passion in the garden, when the apostles were asleep and Jesus said, "Let this cup pass from me"—when he wanted more than anything else to just get out of things—that was the closest I ever felt to Jesus.

They spent the morning in the house like two sick people. Todd didn't get dressed. Joanie didn't answer the phone. They ate cereal. He went back to bed.

In the afternoon he woke up half off his mattress. He could hear Audrey playing "Chopsticks" down in the living room. The radio was on in the kitchen, turned low.

His dog could play the piano when someone held her paws. They'd bought her the piano, a toy piano, as a joke. His mother liked to make her play "Some Enchanted Evening." Audrey had to be in a certain mood to stick it out for any length of time.

He was sweaty. He was in just his pajama bottoms, but he was hot. He kicked off the covers.

He'd had a dream about the Holy Trinity. Jesus had looked thin and pale and seemed too disappointed to speak. God the Father had done most of the talking. The Holy Ghost had been behind them, the way it usually was in the pictures, no help.

He got up. Maybe she'd called. Maybe things were starting to work out, the police on their way.

He was standing at his bedroom door, squeezing the nap of the rug with his toes. He strained to pick up what was on the radio. It changed to an ad jingle.

What he was wearing was suddenly stupid. He wasn't going to be arrested wearing Minnesota Viking pajama bottoms. He changed into soccer shorts and padded downstairs.

His mother and Audrey were playing the piano. She was kneeling, the dog was sitting. They were just plunking around. The piano was half a foot high and had quarter and eighth notes painted on the sides. They were doing one paw at a time.

This was not Audrey's favorite way to spend the morning. When she saw Todd, her tail thumped the carpet.

"There's some breakfast out there," his mother said, concentrating on the keyboard. "I cut up some honeydew."

"What're you doing?" he said.

"Audrey and I're riffing around," she said. "You know. We're just noodlin'."

He went into the kitchen. The radio was on top of the refrigerator. The guy was doing the national news. The local news was after that.

Todd's place was laid out, the honeydew in a Tupperware tub. He thought of the catechism stories of boys tested by God in various ways: one boy gave his lunch money to the beggar with sores, one didn't. One sat down and ate the breakfast he was offered, knowing he'd committed a crime.

He sat down. His mother still hadn't called. He hated that he had to bring it up. He hated the fight they were going to have.

She came into the kitchen and opened the refrigerator door and stood there. She was always after him to not leave the door open.

She had pretty skin, with freckles, and was wearing her hair longer now, down to her shoulders. He liked the color, but she said she was an Italian brunette, like she wasn't happy about it. He watched her mouth while she bit her lip, deciding what to have. He imagined guys she'd meet in the future wanting to kiss her, because she wasn't like some women he'd seen who had almost no lips. She used a little tub of Carmex a lot instead of lipstick, and it picked up the light from the refrigerator door.

She pulled out a box of raisins and a tub of

vanilla yogurt. She always bought something like the seventy-pound size. She spooned yogurt onto his plate and pointed to the honeydew.

"That's enough," he said.

She opened the raisin box and shook it over his plate. Nothing happened, and then they came out in a clump and spattered the yogurt. She got a paper towel and wiped it up.

When she finished, she sat down opposite him.

He didn't eat.

She got back up, poured him a glass of milk, and brought over her coffee mug and a spoon. She spooned coffee from her mug into his milk. She worried about caffeine and he wanted coffee and that was their compromise. He'd liked it also because she'd sometimes make fun of Mass when she did it.

She gave him four spoonfuls. The milk barely changed color.

"You didn't call," he said. She was wearing the same pants from the night before, but a new shirt.

The local news came on. They listened. There was no story about the accident, or any accident. Audrey padded through the kitchen and collapsed near his feet.

"Are you gonna eat?" his mother said.

"Are you gonna call?"

She got up from the table and went outside.

He sat in front of his breakfast, wondering what to do. He wanted all of this to be handled by someone else. He felt like a wind was coming and going on his forehead.

Audrey went to the door, and he let her out and watched to see where she went.

His mother was weeding on her hands and knees in the garden.

The phone rang. He saw her sit up and look back at the house. He thought, Let her get it.

It kept ringing. She was still looking toward the house. He stomped around in little half circles with his fists at his sides and then finally tore the receiver off the cradle.

It was his friend Brendan. "You get it?" Brendan said.

It took him a second: the lacrosse helmet. They'd figured Todd's father would get it for his confirmation. Todd had mentioned it in a letter to his father with that in mind.

It felt like if he was going to say something, he had to do it now, before he kept going with this other life.

It took him too long to answer. Then he said, "The helmet?"

"Du-*uh*," Brendan said. "No. The Uzi. Whadja think?"

Again, it took him too long. "What's *wrong* with

you?" Brendan said. "You get it or not? You didn't get it?"

"Yeah," Todd said.

"Yeah you got it or yeah you didn't get it?"

"Yeah, I got it."

"What colors?" Brendan said, exasperated. "J'ou get any team?"

"White," he said. "It's all white." He pulled the phone cord over to the window. His mother was still sitting up, looking at the house.

Brendan was doing something on the other end while he talked. "I thought you were gonna get Syracuse. You gonna be around?"

"Now?" Todd said. He put his hand over his eyes.

"No, Easter. What 'now'? Acourse *now*."

"I was goin' out," Todd said. He looked around the kitchen, like a lie would be written there for him to say. "I was gonna go do something."

Brendan asked him what. Todd didn't know.

Brendan was getting fed up. Todd put his hand on his hair and rubbed it like he was shampooing, and said to come over now, then.

Brendan made a big sarcastic point about how grateful he was and said he'd be over. Todd wanted to say, You *can't* come over because my mother *killed* somebody last night. He hung up the phone.

His mother was still looking toward the house. He went onto the back porch and cranked open the window.

"Who was that?" she called. He could hear the shakiness in her voice, and he felt like a terrible son, suddenly.

"It was Brendan," he said. He wasn't sure she could see him, with the morning sun on the screen. "He said he was coming over."

She kept looking a minute and then turned back to the garden. Audrey was in her sphinx pose in the dirt between two rows of tomatoes, watching.

He wandered around the house doing nothing.

He sat on the back porch with his hands together.

Brendan took his time. When he finally got there, Todd let him in the back. Brendan walked in and sat at the kitchen table like someone going to a restaurant. He was wearing surfing jams and a white Portland Trailblazers tank top that had a picture of their front line standing there with their arms folded under the words JUDGMENT DAY. He found Todd's dish of M&M's from the night before and ate a few. Todd felt like the M&M's had given him away, somehow. He stood there until Brendan finally said, "So where's the helmet?"

Todd looked at him a second longer and then

realized the helmet was in with all the other presents in the car.

"The helmet," Brendan said.

"It's in the car," Todd said.

Brendan dropped an M&M back in the dish and stood up. He stretched. Todd realized he was supposed to be leading the way. When he didn't move, Brendan gave him another look and headed out the door. Todd followed him.

His mother turned around again and said hello. She waved a little three-pronged rake or scraper. She watched them head to the garage. She peered at Brendan's tank top.

"Where're you going?" she asked Todd. Her voice was a little high.

Todd said he was going to show Brendan his stuff.

"In the car?" his mother said. Did Brendan have to see it now? She started to get up.

But Brendan was already in the garage. He went right to the backseat and opened the door and pulled out the lacrosse helmet. On the floor next to it, he found the Viking helmet.

Todd kept trying to lead him out of the garage. Brendan kept pulling free and going, I can't believe you didn't tell me about the Viking helmet. He put the lacrosse helmet on the hood and tried to pull the

Viking helmet onto his head. Todd could see the dent on the bumper right below the lacrosse helmet.

His mother put her hand on his shoulder. She asked if they didn't want to get out into the sun instead of hanging around the damp, smelly garage. She gave his shoulder a squeeze.

"Let's get out and look at it in the sun," he said.

Brendan was having trouble getting the helmet over his ears, even though it was a large and it was the real thing. He sat up on the hood of the car and held the helmet in front of him by the earholes.

Todd squeezed around to the front and stood by the dented bumper. He wasn't sure what to do with his hands. His mother headed back outside.

"Todd, are you coming out?" she asked.

He reached for Brendan, who pulled his arm away. "Let's sit in the grass," Todd said.

"In a *min*ute," Brendan said. The helmet was half-way on and was squeezing his head like a grape.

"Todd," Joanie said.

"*Ma*—" Todd said. She left the doorway.

"So can you give me a ride Wednesday night?" Brendan wanted to know. He pulled the helmet all the way on and snapped the chin strap. It made his face skinny. He looked around, enjoying the view through the facemask.

"A ride to what?" Todd asked, distracted.

"*Ad Altare Dei*," Brendan said. He was playing with his wristbands. He and Todd always wore wristbands. They thought it was cool. Todd wasn't wearing his. "What's wrong with you?"

"Oh, God," Joanie said, outside the garage. She was out of sight around the corner.

Ad Altare Dei was the religious medal Todd had signed up to go for. All the old altar boys had. You were eligible right after confirmation. It meant "to the altar of God." It was like six weeks of classroom work at night about the Scriptures and catechism, and then interviews with your priest and the bishop, and if you passed you got a medal. They gave it out at a ceremony in front of the whole diocese.

"What'd you, forget?" Brendan said. "Wednesday night's the first night." He was whapping himself on the side of the helmet with his open palm.

"You look sick," Brendan said. "You gonna yack?"

"I gotta get outside," Todd said. "You can stay in here."

He left the garage and sat in the grass. The grass was warm, but the damp came through his pants immediately. He imagined Brendan in there alone, in his Minnesota Viking helmet, noticing something, looking closer at the front bumper.

Nina's car cruised up the driveway, popping gravel on the blacktop. Audrey stood up in the garden and trotted over, barking.

Todd's mother put her hand to the back of her neck. "Just what I need right now," she said.

Brendan came out of the garage.

Nina rolled her window down. She drove with the windows up, even if it was 104 out. She worried about getting colds in places like her ears.

"J'ou hear what happened?" she called to Joanie. She was leaning her head out the window and squinting. Audrey came over to the car and put her front paws up on the door, licking the air near Nina's face.

Todd's mother returned her hand to her side. Her eyes reacted.

"No, what happened?" she said. She turned back to the garden, like she expected to hear Nina say they called off the sale at Stop and Shop.

Nina said it was terrible. Tommy Monteleone: they killed him out on Route 110. Somebody, hit-and-run.

Todd stood there. His armpits sweated.

Brendan sat in the grass next to him. He was trying to eat a KitKat bar through the facemask instead of under it.

Todd's mother turned around. When he saw her

face, he thought it was all going to come apart right then.

"Tommy Monteleone?" she said. "It wasn't Tommy Monteleone." Then she put a hand up to her mouth, as if realizing what she'd done. He looked away. It was like even their mistakes seemed fake, now.

"How do you know? Were you there?" Nina said. She sounded irritated. Todd recognized her tone: *nobody ever listens to me.*

"Tommy Monteleone?" Joanie asked.

"Not *Tommy* Tommy the father," Nina said. "Tommy the son."

"Little Tommy?" Joanie said.

"Little Tommy," Nina said. "Tommy Monteleone. Lucia's son."

Todd's mother stood there, her mouth open a little bit. She braced herself with one leg.

"I know. It's a sin," Nina said. "Terrible. Just terrible. Let's go."

Tommy Monteleone: Todd was trying to picture him. He'd met him twice, maybe, at a wedding and a wake.

She was leaving the car running. What's the rush? Todd thought. Is he still on the road?

It was another one of those times he imagined

God peering down into his soul the way he might peer into an old garbage can.

"I'm going over there now," Nina said. She revved the car, like she was demonstrating. "Let's go."

"Where?" Joanie asked. She shook her head like there was a fly around it. She was still holding the little three-pronged rake.

"Lucia's," Nina said. "Are you all right? C'mon. Let's go."

"I don't think I should go," Joanie said. "Maybe she doesn't want to be bothered—"

"Get in the *car,* you don't think you should go," Nina said. "The woman's boy is run over on the street, you don't want to pay your respects? What do I tell her, you're working in the garden?"

Joanie looked at the garden and then at Todd. "Isn't it a little early? They just got the news."

"They heard last night. We're not gonna stay long," Nina said. "Just stop over. I got some soup and some lasagna. They can heat it up."

"I better change," Joanie said.

"Go like that," Nina said.

"I got dirt all over me," Joanie said. She hurried for the back door. "I'll be one minute."

Inside the house, she called, "Todd, get the dog off Nina's car."

Todd took Audrey by the collar and pulled her down from the driver's-side door.

Nina settled back to wait. She put her head against the headrest.

"Is he going to be able to get that helmet off?" she asked, nodding her head at Brendan. "Wait'll Bruno sees everybody else wearing it but you."

"How did you hear about Tommy Monteleone?" Todd asked.

"I called Lucia, I was trying to organize a bus trip," Nina said. "You imagine? I'm calling about that, her son's dead."

Todd let go of Audrey's collar. She shook herself and stretched and drifted back to the grass. "They know who did it?" Todd asked.

"They don't know. What do they know? I didn't hear a thing about it on the news," Nina said. "Put the dog in the house. You gonna go like that?"

"Me?" Todd said. "I'm going?"

"Sure you should go," Nina said. "It's not gonna kill you. It's a nice gesture. She'll remember. We're only gonna drop the food off."

"Brendan's here, and stuff. Maybe I should stay with him," Todd said. He felt a rush of air that seemed to start at the top of his head.

Nina peered at him. "Did *he* just lose a son?" she

asked. "What is it with you people today? Don't start with me. We're talking five minutes here."

"He just came over," Todd said.

"What's he, live two houses down?" Nina said, exasperated. "Get in the car. Put the dog in the house and get in the car."

Todd grabbed Audrey by the collar without calling her and dragged her toward the house. She thought she'd been bad and went limp, so she was harder to pull. Brendan watched him struggle, with a little smirk.

"Take the helmet off," Todd said, frustrated. "I gotta go."

"Can I keep it on till you get back?" Brendan said.

Todd's mother came out of the house. She looked grim. "Let's go, if we're going," she said.

"Take it off," Todd said. "I gotta go."

"You're going?" Joanie said. "You don't have to go."

"He should go," Nina said. "Don't you start with me now. I just went through all of this with him."

"Ma, what's he have to go for?" Joanie said.

Nina swore.

"You got the other one," Brendan said. "Why can't I keep this one till you get back? You ain't gonna use it."

"Ma, he can't go," Joanie said.

"He can't?" Nina said. "Why can't he?"

Brendan was hitting his facemask with his palm from different angles. Audrey sniffed the air around him to try and sort out what he was doing.

"Get in the car," Joanie said, angry. "Grandma's decided you have to go."

"I'm *go*ing," Todd said. "I'm going."

"So I can keep the helmet till then?" Brendan asked.

"Take it *off*," Todd said.

Brendan yanked it off his head like someone pulling taffy. When he got it off, his ears looked like he'd been out three hours in the dead of winter.

"I'll see you later," Brendan said disgustedly.

"You can come back," Todd said.

"Yeah. I'll get right over here," Brendan said.

Todd got in the car. Nina put it into gear. They backed down the driveway. They passed Brendan, who didn't look up. "Now *he's* mad at me," Todd complained.

"Don't worry about him," Nina said. "Worry about me."

They drove without anybody saying anything. Todd rolled his window down.

The Monteleones lived in Lordship, ten minutes away.

Todd's mother was looking out her window. He was dizzy and a little sick. He had a fantasy that they had the body there and they were going to make him touch it.

Nina adjusted her side mirror, and he could see his eyes. He thought, What you're doing now: this has to be some kind of sacrilege.

"You gotta move outta Milford," Nina said. "You're not near anybody. Milford. You know whose idea *that* was."

She meant it was Todd's father's idea.

They went over the Devon bridge. The metal part in the middle made the noise under the tires he remembered from the Merritt Parkway bridge the night before.

"Lucia said they said he was dead before he hit the ground," Nina said. "He wasn't dragged or anything. Least he didn't suffer."

"Ma," his mother said.

Nina shrugged. Todd closed his eyes so tightly he saw lights behind them.

"How old was he?" his mother asked. She was still looking out her window.

"How old could he a been?" Nina said. "He was born five, six years after you. So what's that make him? Twenty-eight? Twenty-nine?"

They drove on. Bradlees', Spada's Blue Goose Restaurant, Avco-Lycoming Industries.

"It's a sin," Nina said.

"Have they told Perry?" Joanie asked. Perry was Tommy's younger brother. He was in the Navy.

Todd's hands were in his pockets. He heard one pocket starting to rip.

Tommy was coming back to him. He'd been an usher at the wedding. He'd been behind Todd in the line to use the men's room. He'd said something to him. He'd had his jacket and bow tie off and his sleeves rolled up.

"Try WICC," Nina said. "See if they got anything about it."

Joanie fiddled with the stations. She got WICC. The local news opened with contractors and fraud on a municipal project near Seaside Park, a lot of money disappearing. It ended with a mention of the Bridgeport Rosary Society's bake sale, still a week off.

"I don't believe it," Nina said.

They passed Sikorsky Airport and the decommissioned runway. Grass was growing through the cracks in the tarmac. At the light, they pulled up next to a terrier with one of its front legs in a splint, apparently waiting to cross the street.

"They're probably waiting to make sure they notified the family," Joanie said.

"The family knows," Nina said. Todd flashed on all the crying and misery. He imagined himself in the middle of it, responsible.

The Monteleones lived on Spruce Street. There was only the one car there when they pulled in. "She's all alone?" Joanie said.

"Maybe Tommy Senior went out," Nina said. She shut the engine off and opened her door. She waited for a minute, listening. Then she got out. She leaned into Todd's open back window. "Stay here. I'll see if she's in any shape. Give me the box."

Todd handed up to her the carton with the Pyrex dishes of soup and lasagna. She crossed the lawn to the front steps and set it down to get a better grip on it.

"I can't believe this," Joanie said. She put her fingers to the bridge of her nose, and Todd could see them shaking.

"Are we gonna tell them?" he said. But he couldn't imagine doing it. He couldn't imagine anything that was about to happen.

Nina climbed the steps, holding the box with both arms. She tapped the screen door lightly a few times with her foot.

"You didn't recognize him?" Todd said. "When you went over to him?"

"I didn't look that *close*," his mother said. She was upset.

He slid down in his seat, hiding from the house.

"How often have I seen Tommy Monteleone?" his mother said. "Three times in my life?"

The Monteleones' screen door was open, and Nina was handing the box through.

"He had a mustache," his mother added. "The guy we hit didn't have a mustache."

"I don't wanna go in there," Todd said.

"Didn't he have a mustache at the wedding?" she asked.

Nina was talking to whoever was on the other side of the door, probably asking if this was a bad time.

"Of *course* this is a bad time," Joanie said.

"She's probably like you, after Dad left," Todd said. He meant Mrs. Monteleone. "She probably doesn't want to see anyone."

His mother didn't say anything.

The screen door swung closed, and Nina grabbed it. She turned to the car and waved them in.

Todd scrunched down lower. "Ma, we can't do this," he said.

His mother brought both hands together over her face and then moved them apart, rubbing her eyes. She opened her door. "C'mon," she said.

He had his hands between his thighs. She crossed around the car behind him. He thought for a second she'd gone on without him.

She poked her head in his window the way her mother had. "C'mon, sweetie," she said. She needed to clear her throat. "We'll make it. C'mon."

He opened the door and got out and followed her to the front steps. The grass on their lawn was still shaded, so it was wet. The neighbors two houses down had a blue-and-white Virgin Mary, set in a shell in a rock garden. His mother held the screen door for him, but he let her go in first.

The blinds were pulled in the living room. It took a little time for his eyes to adjust.

Nina and Mrs. Monteleone were standing in the hallway off the other side of the room. Mrs. Monteleone had one hand on the sofa back and another on the wall, as if to steady herself. She nodded at them, once.

She had a TV tray set up in front of the sofa. It had a bowl of polenta on it. There was a pat of butter, unmelted, in the polenta. On the lamp table at one end of the sofa there was a big picture of Tommy Monteleone and his brother, Perry. Tommy was in a blue-plaid jacket and tie, and Perry was in his Navy uniform.

"Ma, we're interrupting her lunch here," Joanie said.

"No, come in," Mrs. Monteleone said. She rubbed her temple with the heel of her palm. "You want some coffee? I'm making some coffee."

Todd stayed where he was, a few feet from the front door. Nina waved her hand to tell him to come closer.

"I was just getting some—" Mrs. Monteleone said. She was heading toward the kitchen. She trailed off.

Nina followed her. "Lucia, don't fuss," they heard her say.

"It's already made," Mrs. Monteleone said from the kitchen.

Joanie sat on the edge of a recliner. She gestured with her head toward a big-backed maroon chair near the window for Todd.

"C'mon in here," Nina called.

When they came into the kitchen, she was setting the table with plates next to the coffee cups. She put a glass tray of cookies in the middle and pulled off the Saran wrap. Mrs. Monteleone was scooping coffee into the coffee maker.

"Ma, we don't need anything to eat," Joanie said. "She shouldn't fuss."

"Just cookies," Nina said. "Sit."

They sat. Nina put milk and sugar on the table. She set two cookies on Todd's plate.

"You want some polenta?" Mrs. Monteleone asked.

"We're fine," Joanie said.

Mrs. Monteleone was gesturing at Todd.

"Todd," Nina told her.

"Todd," Mrs. Monteleone said. "Some chicken? I got chicken in there."

"No, thanks," he said. "I got cookies."

She sat at the table, her hands in her lap. The coffee was brewing.

They looked at her. It was like they had to.

"You're sweet, coming over here," she said. She looked at each of them.

Nobody was doing anything or saying anything. Todd lifted one of the cookies on his plate.

"*Tom*my," Mrs. Monteleone wailed. She covered her eyes and started crying.

Todd froze. His mother looked like she was lifting something very heavy.

Nina patted Mrs. Monteleone on the side of the head. She cried herself out after a minute.

She wiped her eyes and got the coffee.

She went around the table pouring it. Todd was still holding his cookie. He put it down.

His mother was rubbing her hands together

like she was soaping them up. "We wanted to say how . . . sorry we were," she said. He felt like he was going to fly apart.

Mrs. Monteleone sniffed and put the coffeepot back on the counter. Nina was looking at Todd and Joanie.

Mrs. Monteleone sat back down. Todd could hear a radio, on quietly in another part of the house.

"Do they have any more news?" Nina said.

Mrs. Monteleone shook her head.

"How's Tommy Senior? He okay?" Nina asked.

Mrs. Monteleone shook her head again. Todd recognized the face: when you don't want to move because you're afraid you'll throw up.

"How could they do that?" she cried. "How could they just leave him there on the road?"

Nina patted her arm and then squeezed it. Todd and his mother stared straight ahead in agony. Todd was looking at refrigerator magnets.

Nina stirred Mrs. Monteleone's coffee for her. They listened to the sound of the spoon in the cup.

They heard a car in the driveway and then a car door slam. They all sat there, everything on hold until this new person arrived.

"Ho," Bruno called from the front door. "Anybody home?"

Nina got up to let him in.

He came into the kitchen carrying a grocery bag. He looked upset. "I got some cake," he said to Mrs. Monteleone. "Dominic's was closed, don't ask me why. I went to Stop and Shop. All they had was Sara Lee."

Todd had no idea what Bruno was doing there. He was emptying the bag: more coffee, a plastic half gallon of spring water, a Sara Lee pound cake. While he put everything away Mrs. Monteleone got up and took some money out of a flour tin in the cabinet and held it out to him.

"Get outta here with that," he said.

"Take the money," she said. "How much was it?"

"Free," Bruno said. "Special sale." She tried to stuff it in his shirt pocket. He took it out of her hand and put it back in the flour tin in the cabinet.

She sat down at that, and sighed.

"How'd you know what she needed?" Nina asked.

"I was over here before," he said. "She said she needed to go out for a few things, I told her I'd do it." He crumpled up the grocery bag with a big noise.

Mr. Monteleone appeared in the hallway. He was wearing an old blue robe and his eyes were impossibly red.

"Hi, Tommy," Nina finally said. "You want some coffee?"

He was wearing black socks and no slippers. He looked over at Todd and then at the sink. He cinched his terrycloth belt and left.

Bruno uncrumpled the bag like he'd done something wrong. Todd and his mother looked at each other.

"He want some coffee?" Nina asked Mrs. Monteleone.

Mrs. Monteleone shook her head.

Bruno went into the dining room and brought a chair back into the kitchen. He poured himself a cup of coffee and then pulled the chair up to the table.

"Where's the other car?" Nina asked. "If Tommy's here?"

"It's in the shop," Mrs. Monteleone said.

The doorbell rang.

"Now who the hell is this?" Bruno said.

"I didn't even hear a car," Nina said. She got up and went to the door. Todd kept his eyes on Mrs. Monteleone, who sat there as if all this was going on in another place.

Nina came back into the hall. "It's the florist," she said. "They won't let me sign for it."

Mrs. Monteleone got up and followed her to the front door.

Bruno spooned two sugars into his cup and stirred it by twirling the cup in his hand.

He was quiet. Todd had never seen him this way.

"What're you doing here?" Joanie said in a low voice.

"What'm *I* doing here? What're *you* doing here?" Bruno said. "I didn't know you knew Tommy."

Joanie shrugged.

"What'd you, just come over with your mother?" he asked.

She nodded. He seemed satisfied with that. He looked at Todd, and Todd thought for a second he was going to ask, You have anything to do with killing him?

He went back to his coffee. "So how'd you know him?" Joanie asked.

Bruno shrugged. "We were friends. We did some business."

"Business? What kind of business?"

"What're you, a cop?" Bruno said. "Business."

Nina came back into the kitchen with Mrs. Monteleone.

"What'd they send?" Bruno asked. "Flowers?"

Nina looked at him. "It's a florist," she said. "Flowers."

They sat back down. Nina got up to warm up

her coffee. It looked like Mrs. Monteleone was going to cry again.

"Ma," Todd said, "can I go outside?"

Bruno slurped his coffee and looked at him over the edge of the cup.

"Yeah, you go out," Joanie said. "We're only gonna stay a little longer. Mrs. Monteleone's got things to do."

He stood up. He didn't know whether to say good-bye or not. Mrs. Monteleone smiled at him.

He went out the way he came in, the front door. He didn't want to have to look at the Virgin Mary, so he walked down the driveway to the backyard. He'd never seen it before.

It was small and fenced in. The next-door neighbor had a yappy little dog that barked at him nonstop as soon as he came around the corner. It clawed at the fence to get at him.

There was one maple tree in the middle of the yard. He sat underneath it. Its roots went so far under the ground they were lifting the blacktop on the driveway ten feet from the trunk.

There was nothing to do. The grass was worn away to dirt at the places where the roots went in. The dog was still barking and scratching at the fence. He put three fingers down to the dirt and brought them up to his mouth.

The back door opened and Bruno and Joanie came out. They walked over to where Todd was sitting. They both had their hands in their pockets and Bruno was jingling change.

The dog was still barking. It was throwing itself against the fence, making the whole thing shake.

"Nice animal," Bruno said, squinting over at it. "They bring a lot to a family, don't they?"

He picked up a stick and threw it over the fence. The dog was quiet, probably checking it out.

"Don't forget, the old man's retired now," he said. "They got nothing. Big Tommy, his idea of savings was whatever was left in the wallet."

Joanie looked back at the house. "Maybe we could help out," she said. "You know, lend them a little bit."

"You?" Bruno said. "Since when do *you* have a pot to piss in?"

Joanie looked down at the grass and then over at Todd. "What happened to you?" she asked. "What've you got on your mouth?"

Todd rubbed it with the back of his hand. "It's dirt," he said.

The dog started up again. They listened to it bark.

"So what do you think?" Joanie said.

"What do I think?" Bruno said. He was looking

off toward the house. "I think I wanna know what happened."

Todd looked at his mother. She had her eyes on Bruno. She shrugged like someone was holding her shoulders. "Maybe the police . . ." she said.

"The police," Bruno said. "Please."

"Well," she said. "Wasn't he just—?"

"Whaddaya *telling* me?" Bruno said. "He's hit by a car wandering around in the dark on Route Oneten?" He exaggerated the pronunciation of the number. He was mad enough that Todd and his mother had to look away.

"This is Tommy Monteleone, now," he said. "This is not a guy who goes on nature hikes. He lives in a rented room on Nichols Avenue. Nature's when a bug gets in the screen."

Todd's mother put her eyes somewhere else. Todd pulled at the tongue of his Nike. The dog was still barking.

"*Shut up,*" Bruno shouted. Joanie and Todd jumped.

The dog was quiet.

"Todd, get up," his mother said. "We gotta go." He could see how shook up she was.

The dog started barking again, hysterically.

"That son of a bitch," Bruno said, looking over at the fence.

"Todd, *come on,*" his mother said. He was up but he was standing around, and she grabbed his shirt sleeve, pinching a bicep. He yanked it free.

"Fine," she said. "You stay here. I'll drive the car up onto the grass to pick you up." She went back into the house, probably to say good-bye and get Nina. He was left standing there with the barking dog and Bruno.

He could feel himself close to crying and fought it. "Bruno," he said.

Bruno looked at him. "What're you, gonna *whine* about this?" he said. "What was she, *mean* to you? Don't whine to me. Those people in the house: *they* got problems."

Bruno walked off. Todd stood there alone, with the barking dog.

What he remembered all through the ride home was the pitiful way he sounded when he said "Bruno." He understood he wasn't thinking about Mrs. Monteleone, or her husband with his blue bathrobe, or the picture of Tommy. He was thinking about the pitiful way he sounded, and the way Bruno looked at him after he said it.

Back in his room, he bridged individual playing cards around the sleeping Audrey. Audrey was on her back with her legs folded in the air. Her head was stretched straight out upside down, and her cheeks hung down from gravity, exposing her incisors. She looked like a sleeping mad dog.

He was using only face cards, leaning them on her side by side, one by one, trying to surround her before she woke up or moved. He had his *Ad Altare Dei* booklet out and was deciding whether or not he would remind his mother. The meeting Wednesday night was at seven.

The booklet was opened to the first page. He'd filled it out when he'd gotten it.

Ad Altare Dei

Record book of	Todd Muhlberg
	221 Indian Hill Road
	Milford, CT 06498

Our Lady of Grace Church
$1.75

He still owed the parish the $1.75.

His mother was in the spare room, next to his, talking to herself.

"What *was* he doing out there?" she said. "What was he doing out there without a car that time of night?"

He'd never told Brendan whether he'd give

him a ride or not. He could call from up here if his mother ever went downstairs. They'd gotten him a phone for his eleventh birthday. His father had been against it.

Going for the *Ad Altare Dei* had been his idea. His mother and grandmother had gone along. Could he drop out of something like that? Could he just not show up?

His mother whacked something wooden in the next room. He heard her get up and go downstairs.

He listened to her bang cabinets in the kitchen. Audrey stirred, and some of the cards collapsed. He kept flipping through the booklet.

Reference Material
Listed below are a few books which will help you prepare for this program:
1. *Old Testament and New Testament*—Confraternity edition.
2. Second Vatican Council:
   Decree on the Church
   Decree on Liturgy
   Decree on the Church in the Modern World
3. *Rite for Holy Anointing*—Liturgical Press. (One dollar.)
4. *Come to Me*—Book Two (the Sacraments and the Mass) Rev. Benedict Ehman and

Rev. Albert Shamon
(Five dollars.)

He stopped reading.

He lay back on the floor, looking up at the ceiling. Sandro had finished it with an overlapping swirl pattern, like a series of waves.

He had to call. He had to call the rectory if he was not going to show up. He couldn't just stay away.

Tears came into his eyes at how complicated everything was. You just feel sorry for *yourself,* he thought. That's all you do.

He sat up again. He had to let them know if he wasn't going. He stood up and padded downstairs in his bare feet. He crossed to the kitchen and opened the cabinet nearest the phone and pulled out the Milford directory.

His mother was sitting at the kitchen table with her back to him. She didn't turn around.

It didn't look like she was making dinner. A colander and a pot were out on the counter, but that was it.

He climbed back up the stairs. His legs were tired. When he came back into the room, Audrey rolled onto her side and looked up, collapsing all the cards. She laid her head down again and closed her eyes.

He listened for noise downstairs and then dialed

the number in the book for the rectory. Maybe he'd get Henry, Father's assistant, instead of Father Cleary.

He got Father Cleary.

"What's up?" Father Cleary wanted to know. "You ready for the big night Wednesday?"

"That's what I wanted to talk to you about," Todd said. "I don't think I can go." His forehead and underarms cooled.

"Why not?" Father Cleary asked. "What're you, sick?"

"No," Todd said. He grimaced at having blown that excuse.

"So what is it?" Father asked after Todd didn't say anything else.

"I don't know," Todd said.

"You don't know," Father said.

Todd didn't answer. Father didn't say anything. He could hear a little buzzing on the line.

"I don't know if it's right for me. I don't know if I should be doing this," Todd said.

"Oh, come on," Father said, surprising him. "You had months to think about this. Now you don't know if it's right for you?"

"I guess I shoulda called earlier," Todd said. He was so dying to get off the phone he did knee bends where he stood, swinging his free hand around.

"Just give it a shot," Father said. He sounded irritated.

Todd tried to figure out what to say next.

"You don't know if you're gonna like it till you give it a try," Father said.

Todd did a knee bend all the way to the floor. He put his free hand on top of his head.

"You do one or two, you decide you don't like it, you can quit with my blessing," Father said. "All right?"

"All right," Todd said. He closed his eyes. It was just like the sacrilege about Communion. "All right."

"Wednesday night. Seven o'clock," Father said. "See you then." He hung up.

Todd turned the receiver around in his hands and put the earpiece against his forehead. He hung up. He could have said it was a mortal sin on his soul he was worried about, and that he'd confess it later, and then later he could have made up something.

He wandered into the upstairs bathroom and sat on the toilet in despair. The phone rang. On the second ring, his mother got it downstairs.

Back in his bedroom, he stood next to his extension, waiting, afraid to pick it up. The click would give him away. But he had to know if it was Father Cleary. He eased up the receiver.

It was Bruno. He didn't notice the click.

Bruno said, "I'm *not* gonna give it up. I am *not* gonna give it up. I told her, 'If there's anything to find out, I'm gonna find it out.' I am *on* the *case*."

"Todd, get off the phone," his mother said sharply. He hung up immediately.

Outside, somebody emptied what sounded like a load of rocks into a garbage can. Todd sat on his bed and folded his hands and looked at the phone, his legs, and Audrey, curled again onto her back, snoring, her incisors still showing.

PART TWO

PART TWO

NINA

IN STRANGOLAGALLI, you lose a man in your family that's it, you wear black the rest of your life. I have a great-aunt over there still in mourning; her husband died in 1944.

Sandro says this'll kill one or both of them, meaning the Monteleones. He thinks they're gonna go to pieces. I tell him maybe the husband. Maybe Tommy Senior. As for Lucia, are you kidding? She's the kind of woman, if there were no fronts on her kitchen cabinets, her kitchen would *still* look neat.

I was thirteen when my father died. He died in August in a heat wave. We sat under the grape arbor he built in the backyard and received the family. One of us had to keep running around the front to get the people arriving, because our doorbell didn't work.

It was the kinda bell you couldn't hear when you rang it, so you didn't know if it was broken and you should knock, or if you should wait to see if anybody came, or what.

My mother was in black. It was so hot the asphalt was soft, and she had a black *sweater* on. I remember flies around her head. She watched us kids play in the tomatoes. It was so hot in there among the stalks you could hardly breathe. And you got the pesticide powder from the leaves all over your hands.

The family gathered around the big cement table, and she sat off by herself. Everyone paid their respects, but nobody wanted to crowd her.

She dabbed at the top of her forehead with a napkin. She watched people come and go. She asked how we could play so hard in the heat, and made us come out of the tomatoes and sit in the shade. She said we were *pazza*. With her dialect it sounded like *pots*. She said even the animals knew better.

The grapes were in, and we ate them off the vine while we sat there. You had to be careful in the big clusters for spiders.

My sister squeezed the skins so that the centers would pop out. Then she ate just the skins.

What I never told anyone was that the week my father died I dreamt he was asking me to go get medicine for him—he couldn't get out of bed—and I wouldn't. And he looked at my face like he knew that I would've gone for my mother.

That was my secret while I sat and ate the grapes.

Poor Lucia. Perry she was proud of, but Tommy—you know. Tommy was the first.

How do we get used to this? That's the secret. How do we do it?

My mother thought here in America the big problems were always just about to get worked out. Polio, TB, influenza, bad roads, prejudice. Someone was off somewhere making new medicines, working out the answers. Our job was to sit tight and hope it happened in time. God protected babies, drunks, and the United States.

In bad times, like when my younger sister got sick with the influenza that killed my baby brother in Italy, my mother would sit in her chair in the kitchen and close her eyes and name the villages surrounding Strangolagalli. Bovile, Ciprano, Monte San Giovanni, she would describe them to herself. We'd tiptoe around the house while she talked about orchards, terraces, and fountains.

When my father died, we waited for her to do that, and she didn't.

She was spotty about Mass afterwards. When the priest would finally see us, he'd take us aside to see if we were okay. What were we going to say?

I was there when he finally cornered her. She'd managed to avoid him for a little while. He told her something about God's will, and she quoted back to him an old Calabrian saying: that God was in charge of everything, but the devil was in charge of the timing.

BRUNO

I WAS RAISED mostly by my aunt and uncle. They're dead, too. My mother, when she went out, it was to pick up something for dinner. My father had a little den and used it.

He was apparently a massive pain in the ass even before they crushed his legs. He got a little money out of that, but how much was compensation then? He hung around the house and listened to the radio and complained. He covered his legs with a blanket even in the summer, and I had to tuck it back in when it slipped off. He drank Old Sunnybrook, this rye that took the print off coasters. The label said, "Takes the wrinkles out of your face and makes your asshole smile." No lie. Look it up.

My aunt told me when he died, "Your father just was never happy, you know? He just never figured out how to be happy." We're standing there at the grave site, and she tells me that.

I was fifteen years old. I felt like telling her, If we knew how to fix that, we'd all be in clover.

My aunt, the one that died, she was best friends with Lucia.

Tommy I knew from when he was a little little kid. He ran a paper-route scam from the time he was about eleven. He'd come by and collect twice for the same week, once from the father, once from the mother. He'd wait until one or the other was out.

My aunt had him figured out early, starting writing down his visits on a pad near the phone. The first time she caught him, she said, "I don't *think* so, Tommy," and he knew enough not to push it. The second time she took him by the hair and brought him inside and showed him the list. She said that at that point he said—his head all twisted around, she's still got him by the hair, eleven years old—that it was his feeling, in a case like this, that the customer was always right.

One thing you had to say about Tommy: this was no lazy guy. This was a young man who could operate. You woke him 6:00 A.M. Christmas morning and put him down in East Dipstick with seven cents, and by noon the next day he had somebody by the balls.

When he wanted to piss me off, he called me Uncle Bruno. He'd go, So you think I should go easier on 'im, Uncle Bruno? You think I should be more patient?

I'd say, Hey, a *cavone* like you, you're gonna do what you want, whatever I tell you.

Lot of people are curious as to what happened to Tommy Monteleone. Let me tell you: a lot of people.

The police, they're like having Andy of Mayberry on the case. They come into the house: Did anybody threaten your son's life recently? Okay, fine, and that's the end of that. They look at this, they look at that, have a nice day, thank you very much.

Old man Monteleone still in his bathrobe; he lost the remote, so he's poking the channel buttons on the TV from his chair with the other end of a broomstick.

One cop actually got interested in the show while the other one was talking to Lucia.

I told Lucia I was gonna find out what happened. She said, "You been a good friend a his all along, Bruno."

That's all true. Though as Tommy would say, So what?

Friendship's friendship and a wonderful thing. But this is money we're talking about. This is *me*.

JOANIE

THE HAPPIEST I'VE EVER been was in fourth or fifth grade. The sisters were always looking out for you, always believed in what you could do. I placed high on an achievement test and instead of moving me up a grade, which I didn't want, they tutored me on my own when things were too easy. That was on their own time. They brought books in extra, and when I finished them, they'd just feed the shelves. I'd do my exercises and then go over and pick out something and sit quietly while everyone caught up. I read most of Dickens that way, and a lot about the Maryknoll missionaries.

They also got me a little encyclopedia I could keep in my desk. I worked my way through it, *A* to *Z*.

They thought I was artistic, so they let me design the bulletin boards. That was a big thing, because the bulletin boards went all the way around the room on top of the blackboards. I had to keep to the basic theme, but other than that I could do anything. In December, we had Advent; in May, something blue with the Blessed Mother in it. In June, the Sacred Heart. They were so nice to me, when I think about it. I'd go to a separate room during subjects I was way ahead in and sit there by myself, drawing pictures and cutting and pasting colored paper.

I won seven straight spelling bees. I was the girls' champion. It was always arranged boys against girls, and the girls would root hard for me. You could see even then that we figured we didn't win many things, so it was good to win those.

I still have the crucifix I got from the seventh one over my old bed at my mother's house. The cross is that fake marble: white with blue swirled through it. The Jesus on it is gold.

Because I was advanced, I was big in the festivals. I loved the Feast of the Blessed Virgin: we all dressed in our white dresses and got to carry flowers. Three or four of us had special parts to say for the congregation. Mine was always "Mary, intercede for us"— three years in a row, "Mary, intercede for us."

I think they connected schoolwork with spiritual grace. If you were advanced in one, you were advanced in the other.

They used milk bottles in the catechism books to

illustrate the various states of grace, like our souls were little refrigerators. Mortal sins looked like bottles of chocolate milk. Saints would have, like, cases of regular milk. I remember I imagined venial sins as pints.

I imagined our souls like white bedsheets instead, with chocolate milk spilled on them. And I remembered my mother saying that after you washed something so many times, it never got so white again.

But making a good confession: you walked out of that church with such a lightness, such a beautiful feeling.

As I got older I got along better with the priests, because I was a wiseass and I was not demure. There were priests who'd like you for that, but the sisters usually didn't.

I'm sorry, now, I didn't get along better with the sisters.

The Monteleones follow me around the house. At night, when I close my eyes, I see the road and Tommy coming out of nowhere.

It's like Nancy asked me once, when she was sleeping with a guy she didn't like, "How'd I end up here? At what point did I end up here?"

I blame Gary. If he hadn't left us, I wouldn't've been driving. It's not fair, but neither is what happened to me. Lying there in the dark, I think all this should be dumped on him. But then I remind myself that he didn't kill anyone and I did.

In every possible situation, now—just standing around, while other people talk—I worry about giving myself away. Behind everything, there's this other life.

This morning I sat on the floor in the kitchen before Todd got up and thought, Hypocrite. Hypocrite. Hypocrite. Hypocrite.

And then at other times—I can already feel it— the guilt goes away. That simple. And I can feel myself living with it the way people learn to live with not being taller, not being more beautiful.

In bed at night I say to myself, I'm not like this. I'm the same as always inside. And that's not true.

So I tell myself, You've got to tell somebody. You've got to go to the police. Tomorrow—tomorrow you'll go to the police.

And then I think about Todd upstairs and think, Will he go to the police?

And I remember the way he looks now when I do something for him: the way the dog looks off to one side when you put her food down, like she's not going to be swayed that easily by something like that.

TODD

I CALLED THE POLICE three different times in the last two days and I haven't stayed on the phone yet. The guy answers and I hang up. The phone's busy and I hang up. The phone's ringing and I hang up.

I called Information in Seattle, Tacoma, and Sacramento, trying to find my father. They found a G. Muhlenberg in Tacoma, but no Muhlberg. I called it anyway.

The guy who answered told me there was no Gary Muhlberg in a three-hundred-mile radius. I musta woke him up.

I called Father Cleary back. I figured I could stay anonymous. Then, when he answered, I hung up, because I figured I couldn't.

I called another parish. I called St. Ambrose in Bridgeport. The woman at the rectory told me that their Father didn't have phone-in hours, and I said what if it was a spiritual emergency, and she said I could come in. I said I couldn't come in, because I was a handicapped guy and the motor on my wheelchair was broken. She said Father could come out to me, what was my address. I told her I lived in another parish. She asked why I didn't go to the priest in my parish. I hung up.

My mother had no idea I made these calls.

I gave up calling. I couldn't think of anyone else to call. I couldn't think of a single other person to call. There was a radio advice guy, but that was long distance and would cost money and my mother would see the bill. There was no one to talk to. I felt like putting a note in a bottle and dropping it out my window. I started writing letters to my dad.

Dear Dad,

How are you? Things here could be better. Mom and I ran over and killed a guy.

Dear Dad,

How are you? Things here could be better. Do you remember Tommy Monteleone?

Dear Dad,

How are you? Mom and I have had a rather rough time lately.

Dear Dad,
    How are you? Mom and I need help.

Then I scratched that out, too. It sounded too desperate. Maybe that was why he left us, because we needed him so much.

I ended up staying up all night. At about two, I snuck downstairs and watched cable. I watched for about an hour. The TV screen was the only light in the house.

Then I thought there might be something about where my father went after Colorado upstairs in all his stuff in the attic. After he left, my mother and my grandmother piled everything of his that didn't get thrown out into a big chest with a lid in the attic. So I went up there.

I didn't even know what I was looking for. A map with a dotted line going from Colorado to some other place? A card from a friend of his saying, If you ever leave your family, come stay with me? Even not knowing what I was looking for, it's amazing how little I found. A bunch of letters he wrote to my mother a thousand years ago. They were wrapped together with electrical tape! I had the feeling she wasn't planning on reading them again anytime soon.

Also a photo of him at the beach. I don't think I was even born yet.

Also at the bottom of the trunk, in a little flat box like you keep Christmas cards in, a satin book that said OUR WEDDING.

I spent the rest of the time I was up there just looking through that. It got light out in the little crappy window covered with cobwebs over the stairs. I found photos of the reception, photos of everyone getting ready. My father looking jokey with two other guys, and a flat metal bottle in his pocket. I found their wedding ceremony they wrote for themselves. With the priest, I guess. Some of the prayers and stuff they didn't write. The rest of the time I was up there, I read along in their ceremony, trying to figure out which words were my father's.

Of course she was going to the funeral. She barely knew the family, saw the deceased twice a year, if that: of course she was going to the funeral.

She'd talked her mother out of picking her up. She was going; that was enough. This way she could come and go on her own, and her parents could stay afterward as long as they wanted.

Todd was staying home. He didn't need to go through that, and not all the kids were going. The official story was that he had a fever.

She'd been up the whole night before. She felt like she was dreaming on her feet. When it got light, she made a pot of coffee, six cups, and drank it all. It didn't seem to have an effect. She stood in front of the mirror at 7:00 A.M., putting on makeup. She tried to work up a little determination. This was her day to become presentable. To look alive. To start to take control of her life. Her eyes seemed half closed.

She put down her blush applicator. She ran her hands through her hair and pulled it back so tight she Chinesed her eyes.

Todd was snoring upstairs in his bedroom. She wiped her hands on her robe, and long hairs spiraled and floated to the floor. She left everything where it was and went up to check on him.

He was across his bed sideways, his feet and arms hanging off. It was already warm, but she pulled the sheet a little more over him. He turned in his sleep and said in a kind of delirium, "It was Wednesday."

She looked around the room. He'd taken his posters down. Pieces of Scotch tape spotted the walls. There was a framed magazine photo of a Minnesota Viking, but that was it. The clean clothes she hadn't folded were in one pile and his dirty clothes were in another. The piles overlapped. There was a map of the western United States taped to the wall by the phone. Colored pins were stuck in various cities. Whether they represented places he thought his father might be or had been, she didn't know.

She went back downstairs and waited for more energy, or for time to pass. She felt thwarted and useless in her own house. She let the dog out.

She must've fallen asleep, or at least into some

kind of daze. Hearing the upstairs shower brought her out of it, and she shook off the grogginess by making another, smaller pot of coffee, decaf for Todd. The phone rang.

It was Bruno. He wanted to know if she wanted a ride to the funeral.

She rubbed her eyes for a while before answering. "I don't," she said. "I want to be able to leave early."

"So do I," he said. "You think I wanna hang around there all day?"

The line was silent. She understood he was waiting her out.

"C'mon," he said. "We can cheer each other up. You're ready to go, we're outta there."

She leaned against the wall, wedging the receiver between her ear and the plaster. "All right," she said. "I won't be ready till the last minute."

While she spoke she wrote notes to herself on the TO DO pad stuck to the refrigerator:

> Coward
> Asshole
> Liar

"Be over in a hour," Bruno said. He got off.

Despite the half-makeup job, she thought she'd better shower. Todd was finished and thumping around his room. She took a shower. He'd gotten water everywhere. When she got out, feeling a little better, he was in the kitchen, buttering a bagel. She sat at the kitchen table, her hair still wet, and combed it out. He brought over the two bagel halves and gave her the bottom. Recently he'd started keeping the best part of the food they shared for himself, as if life without his father made him selfish.

He put marmalade on his half. His face was closed off and concentrating, as if he was counting to himself.

She pulled at a knot in her hair. She had a head-ache. She thought, Is this what it's going to be like from here on in?

"Do you know where Dad might be now?" he said. His lips were chapped and his wet hair looked like a modified punk haircut.

"You mean what city?" she asked.

"Where he is, what city," he said. She could hear the weariness in his voice.

"I know as much as you," she said. "Last I heard, he was heading somewhere in Washington. He never said what city."

Todd tore off some bagel and chewed while squinting at the kitchen window. It was gray out.

"No guarantee he ever got to Washington," she said.

A sports merchandising catalogue was on the floor under the window, swollen and frilled from having been rained on. She could see the circled Minnesota Viking helmet from there.

"You thinking of telling him about what happened?" she asked.

He shrugged.

She got up and went into the downstairs bathroom. While she dried her hair and put on makeup, she tried to think of what to say.

When she came out, he was gone.

She put the dishes in the sink. She got dressed.

She heard him in the living room. She stood on one leg, wrestling with the heel of one of her flats, and peeked in.

He sat on the sofa, bending a spoon into odd shapes. He had the TV on. She couldn't tell what he was watching. It looked like a nature show on rodents. Brown things (beavers? woodchucks?) were rooting around a riverbank.

"You gonna be all right?" she asked. It sounded like she meant, You gonna tell? She felt, suddenly, like an old guard at a tired museum.

"Yeah," he said. He didn't look up. He had the spoon in an S shape.

She heard Bruno's car in the driveway. She said

she'd be back soon and headed out the door. It looked like rain. She grabbed a folding umbrella leaning against the wall near the dog's dish.

The dog was sitting there when she opened the door.

"How long was Sewer Mouth out?" Bruno called, getting out of his car. He'd pulled up on the grass next to the garage instead of parking in the driveway. "All night, I hope?"

"I just let her out," Joanie said. She moved aside to let the dog through and then shut the door behind her.

He watched her walk toward him. "Kid sick?" he asked.

"He's got a fever," she said. She ran a hand through her hair. "What'd you park there for?"

"He looks all right," Bruno said. He gestured up at Todd's second-floor window. Todd was looking down at them.

She could feel herself blush. "What're you supposed to see, fever germs?" she asked. "You ready?"

"You look like you got a fever yourself," he said.

She came around the back of his car and opened the passenger door.

"Can we take your car?" he asked. "Mine's fucked up."

"Why? How?" She hung on the door handle like there was a strong wind.

"How do I know how? It stalled four times comin' over here. Is there a problem?"

"No problem," she said. She turned toward the garage. She felt as if she could not sound, or be, less convincing.

She edged past all the junk inside the garage on the driver's side and opened the door.

Bruno was still outside.

"Well, let's go," she said.

"Back it out," he said. "What am I, gonna squeeze by all that shit?"

She tried to keep her eyes away from the front fender. She got in. All the coffee she'd had came back now, thrumming around inside her. She started the car. It died. She started it again. It died again.

"What is it, going around from car to car? Pop the hood," Bruno said. He came into the garage and edged down the passenger side, his hands on the car body, leaning away from the wall to protect his suit. Shovels and hoes hung on nails, blades outward.

Please please please, she thought. She twisted the ignition once more. The engine turned over.

Bruno stopped, then opened the passenger door as far as he could and wedged his way in.

"Jesus God," he said as a general complaint. She murmured in agreement.

She backed down the driveway, a little fast, she thought. She slowed for the main street. Bruno sighed.

"Things are getting worse and worse," she said. She wasn't even sure how she'd explain the comment if he asked.

"Tell me," he agreed.

She was sweating. She rolled down the window. She thought about where she'd park at the church to hide the front end.

"So how you been?" Bruno asked. He put his arm across the seat and spread out. He loosened his collar. "You been okay?"

"I been okay," Joanie said. She peered ahead like the visibility was bad.

"You talk to the police yet?" he asked.

She took a curve a little wide and overcorrected. "Talk to the police?" she said. "Why would I talk to the police?"

He shrugged and looked back at the road. "Just wondering," he said.

They passed a sign on the side of a parked panel truck: REMEMBER: BEHIND A ROLLING BALL COMES A RUNNING CHILD. It was illustrated with one of those moment-before-the-disaster tableaux: a kid, a red ball, a nonalert motorist.

"J'ou go home One-ten the night of the confirmation party?" he asked.

She looked over at him. He was looking out the window. "I mighta," she said. Her underarms were instantly wet. She was sweating at her hairline, too. "I think I did," she said.

"Yeah, I told the police that," he said. He was still looking out the window. They headed up onto the Devon bridge, and he was looking upriver toward the I-95 overpass. "They'll probably come talk to you pretty soon."

It took her a minute to get hold of herself. She stopped at a light on the other side of the bridge and put her turn signal on. "Thanks a lot," she said. "Just what I need."

"Yeah. Really," he said.

They got going again. She didn't know whether to ask questions or not.

"Hot in here," Bruno said.

She reached awkwardly behind her with one hand and cranked the back window down as best she could. Her arm hurt from the angle and the vehemence of her cranking.

They rode along. She couldn't decide what to say.

"You see anything that night, driving home?" Bruno asked. "A car? Anything?"

She made a show of thinking about it. "No, I didn't," she said.

He made a "that's-too-bad" face.

"Do they think he was robbed, or something?" she blurted. She had no idea if what she was saying was disastrous, but she had to say something. "Did they find anything missing?"

"Actually, they did," Bruno said. "A lotta money."

She looked over at him, both hands on the wheel.

"Keep your eyes on the road," he said.

"He was robbed?" she asked. She couldn't keep the shock out of her voice.

"And you know what?" Bruno said wistfully. "It wasn't his money."

"It wasn't his money?" she asked. "Whose was it?"

"The people whose money it was?" Bruno said. "Very unhappy. Very property-oriented, and very unhappy."

"Whose money was it? How do you know all this?" Joanie asked.

"Whoa, take it easy," Bruno said. "What's the problem?"

She tried to quiet herself down. They stopped again, at a stop sign. She released the steering wheel and flexed her hands. "How much money was it?" she asked.

"This is stuff you're better off not knowing," he said. He looked back over the hood of the car like that was the end of that. "It's clear."

She drove through the intersection.

She didn't know what to do. She had to do something. She had to say something. Did somebody think she robbed this guy? Did he? Was somebody going to come after her for that?

Say something, she thought. You must look like the guiltiest person on earth.

"Be good to get back to church, huh?" she joked. Oh, God, she thought.

"I can't go to church, because I'm a cripple," Bruno said. He watched Spada's Blue Goose Restaurant go by on the left and seemed to check out the cars in the parking lot. "Instead I go to bars."

"You look okay to me," Joanie said.

"My *goodness* is crippled," Bruno said. "My soul is crippled."

The funeral was at Our Lady of Peace. They were coming into Lordship. They passed Avco-Lycoming, and then Sikorsky Airport.

" 'I'm a travelin' man, all over the world,' "
Bruno sang. He had his arm along the door and his
hand on the side mirror.

"Ricky Nelson?" Joanie asked.

"Ricky fucking Nelson," Bruno said.

They drove past Rose Park, which had no roses
in it. The church was across the street. A guy in raggy
long pants and a filthy ORLANDO: WATCH US GROW!
sweat shirt was urinating behind a narrow tree. It was
a pretty small park; he was exposed on just about all
four sides.

"Look at that," Bruno said. "I don't think he ever
got it out."

"Speaking of that," Joanie said, trying for something like banter, "you gonna behave yourself at this
funeral?"

"My ass," Bruno said.

She stopped at the corner and turned into the
church parking lot. The place was jammed. There
was a spot right up front, but she passed on it. She
wanted someplace where she could nose the car's
bumper up against a wall.

"What was wrong with that?" Bruno asked.

"Didn't think I'd fit," she said.

"What're you driving here, the USS *Iowa?*" he
asked.

They circled the back of the church. He made a noise between his lips, like a tire losing air. They turned a corner. It was beginning to look as if there might not be another spot.

"Lotta people here," she murmured. He didn't answer.

"The car's still in good shape," he said.

They turned another corner. She was driving slowly, hoping the funeral would end before they parked.

"C'mon, c'mon," Bruno said. "Grab that other spot and let's go. Somebody else probably already got it."

She accelerated a little. She had to go back out onto the street to circle the building completely. She stopped and put her turn signal on.

"How was it, talking to the police?" she said. "That scares me."

He snorted.

They pulled into traffic and circled around. "It's still there," Bruno said. "Let's go. Grab it."

She turned back into the lot and eased into the space. She had about three feet of clearance on either side. Bruno looked at her.

"I didn't think I'd fit," she said.

Their front end faced the church doors. When

Bruno got out she said, "Bruno," to stop him where he was. She circled around to the back of the car. "Look at this."

"What?" he said. He waited and then walked around to meet her. "What? What'm I looking at?"

"You think I'm gonna lose this license plate?" she asked. "The bolts are all rusted."

He lowered his chin to his chest and looked at her.

"Oh, come on," she said. She hooked his arm and led him down her side of the car. "You'll be my escort."

She tried not to pull when she got past the bumper. He put his hand on the small of her back. "So when're you gonna ask me out again?" she said.

She could feel his eyes on her. She kept hers on the church doors. "Today," he said. "Very soon."

At the entrance she let his arm go and held the door for him. Once he was inside, she glanced back at the car. You could see the dents from there. What she was going to do on the way out, she had no idea.

She followed him into the entryway. Her eyes took a minute adjusting. It sounded like things were just starting. The late arrivals in front of them were dipping two or three fingers into the holy-water font and making the sign of the cross before heading to the pews.

She could tell him she'd hit something. But then why hadn't she mentioned it before?

He'd never go for it. She had to get past this and get it fixed before he saw it.

The church was packed. Everyone was standing for the opening hymn. Bruno pointed out her parents in the last row on the right. They shoved in next to them, nodding their hellos. Her father leaned forward so he could make eye contact and gave her a big smile, as if trying to cheer her up. What did she look like?

She ended up between Bruno and a woman with a newborn baby. The baby opened its eyes wide and closed them. Joanie smiled at the mother, and the mother rolled her eyes.

It started to rain. They could hear it.

Was he playing with her? Had he figured something out? She stood and sat and knelt at everybody else's cue. Could Todd have told him? What was this thing with the money?

"Where's Todd?" Nina whispered.

"Fever," Joanie said.

Nina gave her a look.

Just tell, she thought. It was an accident.

She had to go to the police.

A wind blew through her from some central point. It was just fear of embarrassment that had done all this.

155

She put her face in her hands.

Someone looking at her would have thought it was grief for Tommy.

When the service was over, they held up at the entryway to talk to Nina and Sandro. Bruno was four feet from the front doors and from seeing her car, and was clearly anxious to get going.

A lot of people were standing around, pulling up collars and buttoning jackets. It was still raining.

"We're gonna go out the other way," Sandro said. "We're all the way around the back."

"You going to the grave?" Nina asked.

"Yeah," Joanie said, though they hadn't talked about it. "Could we get a ride with you? No sense taking two cars."

Sandro pointed. "Then we gotta bring you back here."

"Is that such a problem?" Joanie asked.

"She's having some people over, afterwards," Nina said, meaning Mrs. Monteleone.

"Well, we could go over there with you, too," Joanie said. "And then you could drop us off here."

Bruno put both hands up, palms out. "Whatever," he said.

"Sure, fine," Sandro said. "Let's go."

They headed back through the church against the

flow, relief blooming in Joanie all the way down the aisle.

The burial was horrible. It was raining, and people slipped around on the soapy soil near the grave. Sandro almost went down. Somebody in the group behind her was holding an umbrella half over her so that no matter how she moved, the water seemed to be draining down her neck. The priest did everything with thick, sad gestures that took so long that even Nina, shooing mosquitoes with a handkerchief, started to get impatient. It started to really pour. By the time they got back to the car to head for the Monteleones' they were soaked.

"I didn't see Tommy Senior there," Nina said as they headed out of the cemetery. "You see Tommy Senior there?"

Nobody answered. Joanie imagined him still at home in his robe, too broken up to go to his own son's funeral.

They didn't see him at the house, either. They poked around saying hello to some people and introducing themselves to others. Bruno exchanged looks with two guys standing near the TV and nodded. He didn't introduce them.

He followed Joanie into the kitchen. Mrs. Monteleone was supposed to be relaxing, but she was doing a lot of the work. She flexed an ice-cube tray, spread her hand across the top, and turned it over. The cubes fell out onto the floor.

One sister, in from Jersey, escorted her from the room. Another sister picked up the ice.

Bruno was shaking out his suit. He looked like he'd been hosed.

"Fucking *day,*" he said quietly to Joanie, flapping his sleeves. "You want something to eat?"

She looked over at one of the platters. "What is it?" she asked.

"It's Italian, it's meat, and it's free," he said. "That's all you gotta know."

She looked around the kitchen and couldn't believe she was back here again. "You know what?" she said. "I don't think I can take this anymore. I'm gonna go out for like a walk or something."

"It's *rain*ing," Bruno said.

She stood up and ran her palms over her wet hair. "Yeah, well," she said.

It turned out the back porch had a little overhang you could sit under and not get drenched. The front porch was out because that was the way everyone was coming and going.

"You go 'head out there," Bruno said, once she was already outside. "I'll bring some coffee or something. You want coffee? Warm you up."

She said coffee'd be great. She sat on the top step so the door had enough clearance to open without hitting her back. The toes of her shoes were in the rain. She had her elbows on her knees and her hands rubbed her arms.

Bruno came back out with two cups of coffee rattling and tipping on saucers. He held the door with his foot. She took one from him. He'd put cream in hers and added an apricot cookie on the saucer.

He sat next to her. "Get close," he said. They moved together so at least that side would be warm.

"Was that Tommy Senior's brother, with the thing? The harelip?" Joanie asked. "He looked real sad."

"Yeah, he's in mourning," Bruno said. "He just downed a slab a beef coulda served the Flintstones."

Mrs. Monteleone opened the door behind them. She handed forward two lined Windbreakers, one canary yellow and the other white. "You're gonna catcha cold out here," she said. "I got you coats."

"Thanks, Lucia," Bruno said. "We'll be in in a minute, anyway. We just wanted to get some air."

"I got you sandwiches, too," she said. She passed out two packages wrapped in foil. "Eat something."

They took the sandwiches. She shut the door. "You believe her?" Joanie asked. "So good-hearted."

"She wraps 'em in foil," Bruno said.

Joanie put on her jacket and buttoned it up. She helped Bruno with his.

"Thanks," he said.

"Don't want you getting a cold," she said. She smiled at him.

They could hear Sandro in the kitchen right above them: "You kidding me? He charged fi' dollars an hour to build that fence. You could throw your hat through some of the holes in it."

Bruno slurped his coffee and looked around for someplace to put his saucer. He unwrapped his sandwich and took a bite.

She knew she was flirting with him. She knew he was responding. She was trying to figure out how to get more information.

He was peering at his sandwich. "There're like nuts and shit in here," he said. "What'm I eating?"

She looked at her watch. They didn't have anything at home for lunch. She turned over her unwrapped sandwich. Maybe she'd bring it back for Todd.

"So who's the guy you were talking with after church? The guy with the hair?" Bruno asked.

"You jealous?" Joanie asked.

" 'M I jealous. Acourse I'm jealous. You know me this long, you don't know that? I see something

I want, I don't have it: knife in my side. Knife in my side. You know that."

"I'm flattered," she said.

"Miss Coy," he said.

She nibbled her apricot cookie. He was pressing against her from her knee to her shoulder. The rain was letting up a little.

"Great sin, jealousy," he said. "I *run* on jealousy."

"Funny hearing you talk about sin," she said.

"Why?" he said. "What am I? Jack the Ripper?"

She gave him a polite smile.

"He's ascared, that's why," Sandro said from inside. "That's why. He knows they'll come after him."

"I think about sin," Bruno said. "What happened to Tommy Junior: that was a sin."

She closed her eyes. Hail, Mary, full of grace, the Lord is with Thee, she thought. Blessed art Thou among women and blessed is the fruit of Thy womb, Jesus. Holy Mary, Mother of God, pray for us sinners now and at the hour of our death. Amen.

Bruno dropped his sandwich half on the step below him. He put his hand on the exposed arch of her foot, which was cold, and warmed it up. "It's religion I got no use for," he said. "You know? Religion? It's like, 'Repeat after me.' You know what I say? I say,

Why am I repeating after *you?* Who the fuck are *you?*"

She was quiet.

"Sin, I believe in," he said. "The rest of it . . . You hear people talking about be a good this and good that. You hear 'em talking but you don't see it. You know? You want to see an *example.* Mother Teresa? Fine. Where're the rest? I *hear* about saints. All I *see* are Irishmen with red noses passing collection plates."

Joanie cleared her throat and rubbed her nose.

"Don't get me going on religion," he said.

She flexed her toes under his hand. The shoes weren't good, and the rain was going to ruin them. Watch the blue come off on my feet, she thought. She was beginning to feel more depressed than scared, which was saying something.

A police car pulled up the neighbors' driveway. The dog in the house started barking.

A young cop with longish sideburns sat in the car and wrote something on a pad for a minute before turning the ignition off. Joanie was too frightened and surprised to say anything.

The rain picked up again. The cop finished what he was doing and got out of the car. He smiled over at them. He was wearing an elasticized clear-plastic covering on his cap for the rain.

The dog was still barking inside the neighbors'

house. She remembered it was the dog from when Todd was out sitting under the tree.

The cop fumbled with the gate in the fence and then came through into the Monteleones' yard.

"Joey. How are you," Bruno said.

Joanie looked at him and then back at the cop.

The cop pointed at her. "You Joanie Muhlberg?" he said.

She was conscious that her mouth was open. She nodded.

"Sorry to bother you here," the cop said. "I been trying to reach you at home. Nobody answers."

"My son's home," Joanie said. "My son's home now."

The cop shrugged like he wasn't going to explain why the world was so nuts. "Nobody answers," he said.

"So what's the problem?" she croaked. She cleared her throat.

The dog was still barking next door. The neighbors' back door opened. An old woman in a bathrobe leaned out into the rain. "What's the problem, Officer?" she called.

"No problem," he called back. "Sorry to bother you. Just want to talk to this lady here." He pointed at Joanie. The old woman leaned farther out to get a better look.

"Sorry to use your driveway," the cop called. "With all the visitors they got, otherwise I was parking in Stratford Center."

"That's all right," the woman said. She was still trying to get a good look at Joanie. Joanie leaned forward and waved. The woman went back into the house.

"What a dog that woman's got," the cop said.

"Tell me about it," Bruno said.

The cop stood before them just outside of the overhang. Runoff was splashing his foot. "I don't mean to intrude," the cop said. "My name's Officer Distefano. I just wanted to set up a time we could talk."

"What're we gonna talk about?" Joanie said. She clenched her fist at how she sounded.

"This last Thursday night you drove home the route Tommy Monteleone was killed, right about the time he was killed," Officer Distefano said. "We wanted to go over whether you mighta seen anything."

"I already told Bruno I didn't see anything," Joanie said.

"Yeah, well," Officer Distefano said. "Sometimes you remember things you forgot. Sometimes you noticed something you don't think nothing of, we think is helpful."

She looked back at Bruno. He arched his eyebrows in a "get it over with" way.

"Okay, sure," she said. "You want me to come down to the police station? You want me to come now?"

"You don't have to do that," Officer Distefano said. "We'll come to the house. Tomorrow all right?"

She flashed on her car, and Todd. "Tomorrow's bad," she said. She cast around for when Todd might be out. "Tuesday night? Could you do Tuesday night?"

"No, we got that thing Tuesday night," Bruno said.

Officer Distefano looked at him, puzzled.

"That thing? We got that thing," Bruno said.

"Oh," Officer Distefano said. He looked back at her. "Can't do Tuesday night."

She tried to remember: when was Todd's *Ad Altare Dei?* "Wednesday night," she said. "Can you do Wednesday night?"

He said he could. They settled on seven-thirty. Todd was supposed to be at his church thing at seven. The cop told Bruno he'd see him later and then left. He had trouble again with the gate but finally got it. The neighbors' dog kept barking, even after the car had pulled back down the driveway.

They both sat there looking out into the yard.

Low spots were beginning to fill with water. "This weather is something," Bruno said.

"You told him I'd be here?" Joanie said.

Bruno shrugged.

"He's a friend of yours?" she asked.

He nodded and kept nodding, like he'd gone on to thinking about something else.

She felt that everyone knew everything but her, and she was the one with the secret. "Is something going on that I should know about?" she said. She was interlocking her fingers and squeezing them together.

He shook his head and stood up. He picked up his half-finished sandwich and threw it over the fence into the neighbors' yard. Chicken salad flew out of it on the way over. "No," he said, and turned to go back into the house. "There's absolutely nothing going on that you should know about."

When Sandro dropped them back at the car, it turned out that hiding the damage from Bruno was no problem: Bruno seemed preoccupied, and the lot had lousy lighting.

All she wanted to do the next morning was get the car into a body shop. She called around to out-of-town places, garages in Orange, in New Haven, in Hamden, and told them what she needed. She didn't have a ride, so she'd be stuck there. Could they get the parts and fix it today? Most of the places said they'd call her back.

"Why don't you bury the car in the backyard?" Todd said. "Just take it out back and bury it so no one ever knows."

He was sweeping in the kitchen. Every so often he cleaned, to let her know how little she was doing.

She ignored him.

"Or we could like roll it off a bridge into a river," he said.

She held the receiver out to him. "You wanna call the police?" He looked down. "You wanna call the police?"

He set the broom against the wall and left. She thought this was some kind of new low: humiliating her son because he wasn't brave enough to do the right thing.

She sat around the kitchen thinking she shouldn't have told them they should call her back; now she'd have to just sit around and wait. She couldn't go out; she didn't want Todd taking the return calls. She should've told them she'd call them back.

There was a little pile of dog hair and dust in the middle of the linoleum where Todd left it.

"Hello?" Nancy said. She had the back door open. One of her things was coming into the house without knocking. Upstairs, Audrey barked. Joanie heard her jump down from the bed.

"Hey," she called, getting up. "C'mon in." She shook her head bitterly at Nancy's timing, and grabbed the broom and dustpan and swept up Todd's pile.

"Long time no see," Nancy said. "How're you?"

"Okay," Joanie said. "I didn't see you at the Monteleones'."

"You were out on the porch," Nancy said. "I saw you."

Joanie emptied the dustpan into the garbage and banged it to shake the dust free.

"I figured you didn't wanna be disturbed," Nancy said.

Joanie opened the linen closet and hung the broom and dustpan on hooks. "You want a cup of coffee?" she asked.

Sure, Nancy said. She opened the refrigerator and took out the coffee. Joanie took it out of her hand and pulled the coffee maker closer to where she was standing at the counter. Nancy sat down at the kitchen table.

"I had to get out of there," Joanie said. "I couldn't take it."

Nancy nodded.

Audrey padded into the kitchen, head down. She sniffed Nancy and then left the room.

"Great watchdog, huh?" Nancy said.

"You see Bruno out there?" Joanie said. "On the porch with me?"

Nancy nodded again.

"You shoulda come out and said hello," Joanie said. She slopped some ground coffee over the lip of the filter. When she wiped it up with a sponge, it liquefied and produced an unexpected brown smear.

"I didn't wanna intrude," Nancy said.

Joanie made a scoffing noise with her lips. She closed the machine up and turned it on. "You see the cop?" she asked.

Nancy looked genuinely surprised.

"Cop came and wanted to talk to me about Tommy," she said. " 'Cause I drove home on One-ten that night."

"How'd they know that?" Nancy asked. "How'd they find you there?"

"Guy's a friend a Bruno's," Joanie said. "You believe that?"

"Who?" Nancy asked.

Joanie put her head down to think of the name. "Distefano," she said.

"Joey Distefano," Nancy said. "He's nuts about this. He's like Bruno. He's on a mission."

Joanie felt a rising in her chest, like something surfacing. "What does he care?" she asked.

"He was a *good* friend of Tommy's," Nancy said.

Joanie put her fingertips and thumb to her forehead.

"You all right?" Nancy said.

"Headache," Joanie said. "I've had it since last night."

"Jeez. That's tough," Nancy said. Joanie opened

her eyes and looked at her. She had sounded a little sarcastic. Her expression looked sympathetic.

"You know anything about Bruno and Tommy?" Joanie asked. She turned back to the counter and got out mugs. "You want Danish or something? We got a little Danish in there."

"What do you mean?" Nancy asked.

"Were they good friends? Did they, like, work together? I didn't know they were so close."

"They both worked for that guy outta Bridge-port," Nancy said. "Joey D, too. He was moonlight-ing."

"What guy?"

"That guy, you know," Nancy said. "Ran the scrap-metal place. What's-his-name."

Joanie turned to face her. "I don't know. What's his name?"

Nancy shrugged.

"What're you tellin' me?" Joanie said, exasper-ated. "They all sold scrap metal?"

Nancy made a "don't be a wiseass" face.

They heard a car door. Nancy stood and leaned over the table to look out the kitchen window. Her expression changed completely, and she flopped back into her chair. "Your boyfriend's here," she said.

"Oh, for God's sake," Joanie said.

"*Ho*," Bruno called from the back door. Audrey barked. "*Shut* up," he said.

The dog ran up to him, sniffing and swinging her rear end back and forth. "Get away from me, you sack of shit," he said mildly, rubbing her head. He pushed past her into the kitchen, his thigh sweeping her aside. He noticed the new washer–dryer she'd just put in and he ran his hand over it.

"Thought I'd stop by on the way to the dealership, see how you're doin'," he said. He looked over at Nancy. "Well, isn't this nice," he said. "The girls're havin' coffee."

"Hi, Bruno," Nancy said.

"Joanie? Hello?" Bruno said. He lowered his head to peer up at her.

"Bruno, how are you," she said.

"I'm not gonna take up your time, here," he said. "You got things to talk about, girl things. Feminine hygiene. I just wanted to remind you about what you said."

Joanie looked at him. "What'd I say?"

"You wanted to know why I wasn't asking you out. And I never did. So now I am."

Nancy looked down at the floor. Joanie looked away.

" 'Less you changed your mind," Bruno said. "Came to your senses."

172

Joanie didn't answer. Bruno stood there with his hands out, like he was waiting for something he was due. The coffeepot finished bubbling and spitting.

"Bruno, your timing is something," Joanie said quietly.

"No, it's all right," Nancy said.

Joanie brought the coffeepot over and poured Nancy coffee.

"I got a boss waitin' on me, here," he said.

"Bruno," Joanie said.

He put his hands wider apart. "I'm a slave for love. I admit it. I humiliate myself in front of other people—I admit it."

"You want cream?" Joanie asked. Nancy shook her head.

"You think about it," Bruno said. "You get back to me."

Joanie put the coffeepot back into the maker. The phone rang. Bruno picked it up and handed it to her without saying hello.

"Hello?" Joanie said.

"This is J and L Gulf," a voice said. "We can get the parts two a clock, two-thirty this afternoon."

Joanie cupped a hand around the mouthpiece. Bruno dropped his mouth and raised his eyebrows in a comic way. "Look at Secret Spy over here," he said.

"So it's okay?" Joanie asked.

"Yeah. Yeah, you bring it in, we'll get it done," the guy said.

"I don't think I want any coffee," Bruno said. "I gotta get going, anyway."

"Nobody offered you any," Nancy said.

"No kidding," Bruno said.

"Though you take it away today, you're gonna take it away wet," the guy on the other end said. "Long as you know that."

Joanie pursed her lips, thinking.

"Hello?" the guy said. "You comin' in or not?"

"Yes," she said. "That's all right." She hung up.

"Ask Bruno about that guy," Nancy said.

"Nancy," Joanie said.

"What guy?" Bruno asked. He opened the pastry box on the counter near the refrigerator and looked inside.

"Joanie wanted to know about that guy you and Tommy worked for."

Bruno looked immediately at Joanie.

"I was curious how you knew Tommy, that's all," she said.

Bruno shook his head. He lifted something in the pastry box and let it go again.

"Why, is he a mob guy or something?" Joanie asked.

Bruno made a disgusted noise and shook his head again. "Movies," he said.

"Is that it?" Joanie asked.

He turned to face her and scared her a little. " 'Mob guy'? What is this, the *cinema?* What are you, the G-man? You asking me if this guy is legitimate, one hundred percent? I say: No, he's not. I say to you: Not many people *are.*"

"I'm just *ask*ing," Joanie murmured.

"You're *not* 'just askin'. You say to me: What does he do that's *not* legitimate? I say to you: None of your business. Here's a good rule of thumb if you want to do something that's not legitimate: Keep it *quiet.*"

The phone rang again. Joanie answered it. It was a garage in New Haven: they'd found the bumper but not the grillwork. She told them it was all taken care of, anyway.

"Gettin' a lotta short phone calls," Bruno said when she hung up.

Todd came into the room and opened the refrigerator.

"Man o' the house," Bruno said.

"Hey, Bruno," Todd said, his head in the refrigerator.

"Hello, Todd," Nancy said.

"Hello, Nancy," Todd said.

"Todd know his mom's bein' questioned by the police?" Bruno asked.

Todd froze behind the door. The shifting and sliding sounds of his search stopped.

He stuck his head up and looked at Joanie.

"A friend of Bruno's," she said. "That's all. He just wants to go over what they already know."

She was about to say something else to reassure him, but the phone rang again. She made an enraged sound and snatched it up. Bruno chuckled.

It was the Orange garage. They couldn't do it today, or tomorrow, either.

"So how's *your* memory about drivin' home that night?" Bruno asked quietly.

Todd spooned vanilla yogurt from the tub into a dish. He shrugged. His face flushed.

Joanie told the garage it was already taken care of.

"Todd," she said. When Todd looked at her, angry, she said, "See if anyone else wants some."

"None for me," Bruno said. "Yogurt? Holy God."

"Lemme make sure we're canceling the right party here," the voice on the phone said. "This is Mulenberg?"

"Muhlberg, yes," she said. Bruno looked at her,

and she rolled her eyes and circled her index finger near her temple.

"Muhlberg?" the guy said. "Not Mulenberg?"

"Poor Tommy. Terrible thing," Nancy murmured to Todd. He nodded, but he couldn't look at her.

"Muhlberg, Mulenberg, cancel them all," Joanie said. She had to go; thank you. She hung up.

"Subscriptions," she said to Bruno.

Todd stood in the doorway to the hall and ate his yogurt. "So when are you gonna be questioned by the police?" he asked.

"Sit at the table," Bruno said. He was leaning against the wall with his arms folded. "You're gonna get indigestion."

"These kids don't care," Nancy said.

"Nobody gave Bruno any coffee?" Todd said.

"We never got Todd's side of the story," Bruno said. "You're a passenger, you see a lotta things the driver misses."

The phone rang again. Joanie swore.

"Get me a copy of *Field and Stream,*" Bruno said. "And get a copy of *Modern Bride* for Nancy here."

"Fuck you, Bruno," Nancy said.

It was Nina. "Who's over there?" Nina said.

"What happened to 'Hello,' Ma?" Joanie said.

"What's *your* problem?" Nina said. "I just asked who's over there."

"Nancy," Joanie said. "And Bruno."

"Who's that? That your mother? Send her my love," Bruno said.

"What'd he say?" Nina asked.

"He said he's sorry he's always rude to you," Joanie said.

"Tell him not to get fresh," Nina said.

"Don't you hafta be at the dealership?" Nancy asked. "Shouldn't you be cheatin' some widow out of her life savings at this point?"

"Yeah, I gotta go," Bruno said. "Todd, Yankee game: tomorrow night?"

Todd blinked, still holding his yogurt dish. "At the Stadium?" he asked.

"No, at my house," Bruno said. "I'll buy chips. *Acourse* the Stadium."

"When did this come up?" Joanie asked, a little panicked. "When'd you get this idea?"

"When did what come up?" Nina asked.

"Hold on, Ma," Joanie said.

"What?" Bruno said. "Just now. You heard it."

"I got *Ad Altare Dei* Wednesday," Todd said.

Bruno shrugged and turned his head slightly to

178

the side. "And I'm busy Christmas Eve. But I'm talking *tomorrow* night here."

"Okay. That'd be great," Todd said.

"I'll pick you up six o'clock," Bruno said. "We'll get something down there."

"Are you still there?" Nina said. "Hello?"

"I'm not sure about this," Joanie said, trying to get Todd's attention.

"Thanks for your input," Bruno said, heading for the door. "I'm outta here. Tell your mother she drove me out of the house."

"She'll be thrilled," Joanie said. "Ma, you just drove Bruno out of the house."

"I'm thrilled," Nina said.

Bruno pointed to Joanie. "You think about where *you* wanna go. Remember, the date was your idea." He had the door open and he pointed to Nancy. "Nancy. Hang in there."

"Fuck you, Bruno," she said again.

Bruno spread his hands wide for Todd. "I come in, I'm polite, I get shit on," he said. He went out the door whistling.

"Nancy," Joanie said.

"Well, he pisses me off," she said. "Rubbing my face in it."

"I know," Joanie said.

"Rubbing your face in what?" Todd asked.

"Todd, leave it alone," Joanie said. He tossed his empty dish and spoon onto the counter with a clatter, and turned and stalked off.

"Is he getting fresh?" Nina said.

"Ma, come over if you wanna talk," Joanie said, exasperated. "Between you on the phone and everybody, I'm goin' nuts here."

"Pardon me for living," Nina said. "Good-bye and good luck." She hung up.

Joanie looked at the phone and blew out some air before hanging up.

She turned to face Nancy. She wanted to get rid of her so she could talk to Todd. She didn't want to imagine Bruno working on Todd for four hours at a baseball game, and they had to figure a way to get out of it.

"So what d'you got planned for today?" she asked Nancy. "You want more coffee?"

"Sure," Nancy said. "Pisses me off when he does that." She handed her mug to Joanie.

"Bruno's Bruno," Joanie said.

"Well, that's helpful."

"Well, it's true." She poured what was left in the coffeepot. "There's only half a cup here."

"Make another pot," Nancy said.

Joanie closed her eyes, her back to Nancy, and rubbed her face. "I think I'm out," she said.

"No, you're not out," Nancy said. "I felt the can."

Joanie grabbed the can and ripped off the lid.

She heard Todd on the stairs and then at the front door. "I'm goin' out," he called.

"Todd?" she called back. "Todd?" She leaned sideways to see down the hallway. "Where you goin'?"

"Out," he called. The front door slammed.

"Ah, they're something, aren't they?" Nancy said. She sighed.

"Hold on a sec," Joanie said. She hurried to the front door. She swung it inward and looked both ways down the street. He was already gone. Had he gone around the side of the house?

"How could he disappear that fast?" she said, coming back down the hall.

She sat at the table, after starting another pot of coffee.

Nancy was the last person she needed to deal with right now. "I'm real busy," she said.

Nancy looked down.

Come on, Joanie thought. This is your best friend.

"Hey," she said. "How're you doin'?"

Nancy leaned forward in her chair and put her elbows on her knees. She gave Joanie a little smile and looked down the hall toward the living room. "You heard anything from Gary?" she asked.

Joanie wanted to help, but she didn't have time for this. And she was worried about Todd. "Don't worry about Bruno," she said. "He's all talk."

"I didn't just bring it up because a Bruno," Nancy said. "I been thinking about you."

"Thanks," Joanie said, but she didn't sound as touched as she felt.

They both were staring down the cluttered hallway.

"You're really letting the house go," Nancy said. She sounded sad rather than judgmental, but Joanie was still a little offended.

Joanie got up and poured their coffee. She pushed the half-and-half closer to Nancy's cup with two fingers.

"We gonna talk, or what?" Nancy said.

"What're we doin' now?" Joanie asked.

Nancy snorted.

They went all the way back to junior high. Joanie remembered a night before a Spring Fling dance, the two of them improvising to disguise the little cycle of good dance clothes they owned.

"The Gary thing got me down, and . . ." She

searched around for something else. She was terrible at this, even when she was telling the truth. "Bruno's been a pain."

Nancy looked away.

"I'm sorry," Joanie said. "You know what I mean." What she meant was, I'm sorry about the way you feel about Bruno.

Nancy nodded. Joanie thought, This is a woman who never got one break.

She had another memory, from after high school: the two of them showing each other their diaries. She remembered thinking it was their way of proving to themselves that someone in the world might be interested. She remembered Nancy used little symbols, a code for herself. To make it more exciting? To save time? As a kind of modesty? Joanie couldn't tell. She remembered some of the bigger ones: Three wavy lines meant depression. A skull and crossbones meant sex.

"I put up with so much shit from him," Nancy said. "Like just now. He has to do that in front of you? He has to ask you out in front of me?"

Joanie gave her a sympathetic look, but she could feel her concentration slipping back to the car in the garage, Todd wandering by a police station.

"I should get one of those books," Nancy said. "*Women Who Love Guys Who Love* . . . whatever. I went to a bar the other night. Mr. P's. I called you but you were out. The night a Todd's party, after we all went home. I just thought, you know, I don't need anybody to go out with. I took a booth, I'm minding my own business, Bruno comes in with Joey Distefano and two other guys."

Joanie sat up. "Joey Distefano?" she said.

"The cop," Nancy said. "You met him. Bruno sees me, you think he comes over? You think he introduces me? He just starts joking." She was lifting her mug and setting it down with her middle finger and thumb.

"What'd he joke about?" Joanie finally said quietly.

Nancy lowered her head, ashamed, and Joanie felt a pang for asking.

"Like he thought I couldn't hear him," Nancy said. She lifted her mug and set it down again. "So I drank three beers so I could make my own jokes," she said.

From the living room they heard the jingle of Audrey's tag as she scratched herself and the grunt when she collapsed back onto the carpet.

Joanie touched her hand to Nancy's upper arm. "Sweetie," she said.

Nancy stood up. "You know what? I'm gonna let you do whatever you have to do today."

"You want another cuppa coffee?" Joanie said.

"You're busy, I'm busy," Nancy said. "Gimme a call sometime. I gotta roll." She squeezed Joanie's shoulder. When she opened the back door, she called, "Audrey. Break-in in progress," and waved to Joanie before shutting it behind her. Audrey didn't bark.

She washed out the coffee cups and put them in the dishwasher. It was already eleven-thirty. She made a nice sandwich for Todd, pepperoni and cheese. She cut it in half and sat next to it for a moment, like it was her accomplishment for the day. She covered it with a napkin.

She was all jittery. She had a three-hour wait before she could take the car in. If she left a little early, two and a half hours.

At some point she should eat. She made herself a half sandwich, of provolone only, and fed it to the dog.

She cleared out the hall. She swept upstairs in the spare room and found on the floor a half-filled mug of coffee that had to be a week old.

She called Brendan's house. Todd hadn't been there.

Audrey followed her from room to room.

She went out to the garage and squeezed past all the junk up to the front of the car. She studied the dents. She was trying to think of what to claim she hit. First she thought a pole. Then she realized there'd be scrapes, that the paint would look different and the dents would be less gentle. A bush? A deer? Did they even ask when you brought a car in? Still, she had to have something ready, even if they just asked casually. What would she say? None of your business? She got impatient with herself and left the garage.

She wrapped Todd's sandwich in foil and put it in the refrigerator at the front of the top shelf.

She sat back down at the kitchen table. Did he have any money for lunch?

The phone rang. When she answered, nobody was on the other end.

She thought about how unhappy Nancy was, how little help she'd been. "When was I ever any help?" she said aloud.

Audrey pattered into the kitchen, assuming she was being talked to.

Those things they put near highway exits. Those barrels filled with sand: she could say she hit one of those. She tried to anticipate ways in which someone could figure out she hadn't.

The kitchen clock made a small clicking noise. She scratched her instep with her heel. Her stomach was churning. On a scratch pad on the table she drew an oval, and put two dots inside it and gave it a smile.

She drew a parody of her hair. She wrote JOANIE underneath it and crossed it out with a single huge *X*.

She went back out to the garage and checked the roof of the car. He'd hit the roof of the car. She got her eyes low to the roofline and saw the dents: wide and shallow, at least two. They were hard to see, maybe because the car was a dark color.

She put her hand on one, like she could still feel body warmth.

There was nothing she could do about those. What was she going to say? She hit one of the barrels and it bounced over her head?

She squatted beneath the junk on the wall. She was never going to be able to relax. The roof was always going to be like this. A year from now she could see Bruno running a hand over it and suddenly looking at her.

She calmed herself down. He hadn't seen them yesterday. Neither had she.

She went back inside and watched TV, trying to figure out what to do. She was waiting for Todd and two o'clock. "The Andy Griffith Show," "The Dick Van Dyke Show." Rob's boss had a toupee and something funny was going on with their not wanting him to know they knew. Two o'clock came first.

She tore off the top page of the scratch pad. On the page underneath, she wrote, *Todd—Back soon—*

Sandwich in Frige. She swore and jammed in a *d*, making it *Fridge*. She added, *Want to go to a movie tonight? Love, Mom*, and centered the note on the table.

Want to go to a movie tonight? she thought acidly, backing down the driveway.

She wandered around Hamden for twenty minutes looking for the garage, unwilling to ask directions, as if that were the clue that would give her away. When she finally found it, the guy came out to see her, rubbing his hands with an oily black rag. He flapped the rag toward one of the bays, and someone else guided her in over the lift. She sat in a paneled waiting room while they worked. No one talked to her. New radial tires on stands were angled around as decorations. She sat near a table covered with *People* magazines that looked like they'd been dumped out of a box.

While they were still working on her car the guy she'd talked to on the phone called her over to the cash register. The bill was four hundred and something. She took out her checkbook. It occurred to her that she should've paid cash, so that no one could trace the check. But maybe paying in cash would've been suspicious to this guy.

He took her check and thanked her and told her the car'd be out in a few minutes. He reminded her that it wouldn't be completely dry and that she'd probably get grit in the finish.

She sat back down. It was almost four.

One of the guys who'd worked on the car looked into the waiting room. When he saw her, he came over and dropped a quarter in her hand.

"What's this?" she asked.

"Good-luck quarter," the guy said. "We found it when we pulled off the bumper. Musta dropped down where the grillwork got pushed against the chassis."

She stared at it in her hand.

"Car's all set," he said. "If you're sure you don't wanna leave it overnight."

"Thanks," she said. When he left, she slipped the quarter inside one of the *People* magazines and burrowed the magazine deep inside the pile.

Todd wasn't back when she got home. She called Brendan, and Brendan's mother still hadn't seen him. Was everything all right? Everything was fine.

She sat staring at the phone. He didn't have a lot of friends.

She called another kid he'd gone to the movies with once. The kid was out, but his mother was sure he wasn't with Todd.

She didn't know what to do while she waited, where to look. The kitchen had a faint cinnamony smell. She called Bruno. She wanted to tell him she'd go out with him.

"Hey, there. Todd's over here," he said.

"Todd?" she said. She was standing, and she leaned back against the counter. "Over there? How'd he get over there?"

"I saw him wandering around, I picked him up. Why? Were you worried?"

"Of course I was worried," she said. "I didn't know where he was. Where'd you pick him up?"

"So anyway, what's up?" Bruno said. "You callin' to look for him?"

"No," she said. "Put him on for a second."

There was some muffled fumbling and talk. Todd gave a low laugh.

"Hello?" Todd said.

"Hey, you," she said. "Why didn't you tell me you were going over there? I was worried."

"I didn't know," he said.

"Why didn't you tell me, once you were over there?"

He didn't answer.

"Did you eat anything?" she asked. It was all she could think to say.

"Bruno says we're gonna go out," Todd said. The receiver was muffled again and Bruno said something and they both laughed.

"What d'you mean, out? You mean for dinner? It's four-thirty," she said.

"Hold on a sec," he said.

"Todd?" She clapped an open palm on her thigh in frustration.

"What's up?" Bruno said.

"What's up? You got my son all day, I don't know where he is, and now you want to go out. I gotta feed him dinner," she said.

"Yeah, we're goin' out, get something to eat," he said. "We'd ask you along, but it's a guys' trip." Todd said something she couldn't hear. "The guys're gonna do some talkin'," Bruno said.

"Bruno, let me talk to him," she said.

"Hey, hey, hey," he said. "Everyone remain calm here." His voice got faint, and she imagined he was holding the phone out to Todd. "Your mother wants to say good-bye."

" 'Bye, Ma," Todd said in the same faint voice.

"He says 'bye," Bruno said.

"Bruno—" she said. She was holding the receiver with both hands.

"You said you weren't calling about Todd," Bruno said. "So what were you calling about?"

She raised her toes and insteps so that she stood only on her heels, and then flopped her feet back down again. "I wanted to let you know we could go somewhere sometime," she said. "Lemme talk to him again."

"Your mom and I are going on a date," she heard him say. She winced. "That's great," he said. "How about this Saturday?"

She thought about it, distracted. She still wanted

to head off the baseball game. "How about tomorrow night?"

"Tomorrow night? Tomorrow night I can't. Tomorrow night I got the baseball game with my pal Todd here." He coughed. "She wants me to go tomorrow night," she heard him say to Todd.

She waited. Out the kitchen window, she could see a neighbor hefting a huge black trash bag into a can.

"For you, we're flexible guys," Bruno said. "Also, because we haven't bought the tickets yet. But it's gonna cost you. Todd says you gotta show me a good time."

"I didn't say that," she heard Todd say.

"Put him on," she said.

"I'll pick you up tomorrow night, six o'clock," he said. "I don't know what we'll do yet, but I'll think of something. I got connections."

"Bruno, put Todd on," she said.

"See you tomorrow," Bruno said.

There was the woolly sound of another phone exchange. "I'll be back around six," Todd said.

"You gonna be all right?" Joanie said. "You got any money?"

"No," Todd said.

"Well, you keep track of what Bruno spends so I can pay him back," she said.

"Yeah," he said. He waited.

"You mad about giving up the baseball?" she said.

"We're not givin' it up. We're goin' on Tuesday," he said.

"Tuesday?" she said. A headache she'd been aware of for a few minutes felt worse. "I thought it was tomorrow."

"It is tomorrow. And Tuesday. It's a three-game series," Todd said.

"Put Bruno on," she said, gritting her teeth.

"He says he's already out the door," Todd said.

"Todd—" she said.

"We gotta go," he said. "See you soon." He hesitated and then hung up.

She held the receiver away from her and pitched it toward the kitchen table. The cord pulled it off the table and across the floor. It ended up near the dog's dish, swinging back and forth on one end. The off-the-hook beep started.

Audrey furtively climbed the stairs, probably assuming she'd done something wrong. Joanie stood there with her arms folded until the beeping noise annoyed her enough. Then she replaced the receiver, poured herself a glass of orange juice, and ate the sandwich she had made for Todd.

———

Todd didn't come home at six. He came home at eight. Joanie was watching videotaped footage of her wedding on the VCR when he came in. She'd been digging around looking for a tape they'd made of Todd as a baby—Gary holding him on his lap when he was eight months old and drumming his arms at high speed to Benny Goodman's "Sing, Sing, Sing." They called it "doing his Gene Krupa." She loved the way he looked up at the camera and laughed his big, short, baby laugh.

But she hadn't found it, digging around on the closet floor. The tape she'd found that she thought might be it turned out to be her wedding tape, made by a relative with shoes so squeaky it sounded like someone was playing with a child's toy throughout the ceremony. Once it was on, she let it go, a little stunned by the unpleasantness of watching it again. It opened with a misspelled greeting from the filmmaker: BONA FORTUNA GARY AND JOANIE. Then there was snow and a glimpse of something involving a knife that had apparently been on the tape first. Then guests arriving. A champagne bottle. Her own back while she flounced comically for her friends. Gary's father standing by a tree, looking glum. The guests inside the church, the video golden and grainy. Gary and his best man waiting in the priest's chambers, holding up a hip flask and mugging. Jagged pans, a disorienting swoop past something, overexposed stained-glass windows, someone's feet. A group of Gary's relatives who'd come from Pennsylvania. Behind them, off by himself, Bruno, looking grim.

"What're you watchin'?" Todd said behind her.

She hit the stop button on the remote like she'd been caught with pornography. The regular programming appeared, a sitcom. He looked at her suspiciously.

"Where've you been?" she asked. She'd coached herself on her tone while she waited: casual but concerned. It came out a little higher pitched.

"I told you," he said. He left the doorway.

She got up and followed him upstairs.

"We went out to eat," he said, without looking back. Audrey was following her now, too, the three of them trooping up single file. He walked into his room and swung the door half shut behind him. She pushed it open.

"Ma," he said.

She had her hands on her hips. "You were eating all this time?" she said.

"I was with Bruno."

"I was worried," she said. The dog sidled by her into the room and walked over to Todd.

"Because I was late, or because I might tell someone?" he said.

The dog lowered her head and walked back out of the room.

He looked away. Joanie was staring at him. "Don't you talk to me like that," she finally said.

"I'm sorry," he said. He turned on the stereo atop his dresser and sat at his desk. There was already a record on the turntable.

She watched the tone arm go up, over, and down. Some music she didn't recognize started.

"Did you talk about that at all?" she said. "Did he ask you questions about that night?"

"No," he said.

"Todd."

"He *didn't*. I'd tell you. Okay? I'm as guilty as you are."

"Todd," she said, shaking her head.

"I wanna listen to this."

She stood there. The music was turned way down.

"Where'd you go?" she asked.

"Spada's."

She folded her arms. "You were eating all this time?"

He turned up the stereo. She crossed the room to it and hit the cue button. The tone arm lifted.

"Ma," he said.

"I said, were you eating all this time?"

"I had to wait while he talked to this guy."

Outside the window, somebody's starter motor made a grinding noise. "Who?" she asked. She was afraid she already knew.

"Joey Distefano," he said.

She sat down on his bed. "Todd," she said. "Listen to me. Something's going on. I don't know what."

"Are you gonna do this every time I go out now?" Todd shouted.

She stared at him, her hands together in her lap. She closed her mouth.

He shook his head and wandered around his room. "Could I have my room?" he said. "Could I have my privacy?"

"Todd," she said. "This guy and Bruno are trying to find out what happened that night. I'm not sure why."

"Maybe they just wanna know who killed their friend," Todd said.

She was shaking. She took a breath. "Something else is going on. You *can't* talk to them about it. You understand?"

He went to the window and leaned on his outspread arms and lowered his head.

"*Do you understand?*" she said, raising her voice.

"*Yes.*"

She sat there, unsatisfied. She wanted to let him alone. "You didn't talk to him about that night at all?"

He started to cry.

She went to him immediately and tried to get an arm around him, but he pulled away. "Okay, honey, okay, I'm sorry," she said. "I'm sorry, honey," she said, and backed out of the room. She was in the hall only a second before he shut the door behind her with a bang.

He was gone the next morning when she got up. His bike wasn't in the garage. She thought about calling Brendan's house but imagined getting his mother again. The dog apparently had eaten something outside and had thrown it up on the living-room rug, a discreet greenish mess. She spent a half hour cleaning it up.

Her mother called and invited her out to the mall. She didn't want to go. Nina stopped by, anyway, and talked her into it. For three hours they wandered around. Joanie sniffed her hand occasionally, sure she could smell both the ammonia and the dog barf. They had lunch at Taco Bell. Across the atrium, she spotted Joey Distefano out of uniform, sitting by himself and having an ice cream.

When they got home Todd was still out, but he'd

been back. A plastic knife covered with peanut butter was in the sink. Otherwise, he'd cleaned up after himself. Nina asked where he was. Joanie said she didn't know.

They sat around talking for an hour. Joanie made coffee. Her mother sniffed the air and looked around uncertainly. You could still smell a little of the vomit. She sniffed her coffee cup.

She asked what Joanie was up to tonight. Joanie shook her head, like it wasn't even worth talking about. She didn't mention the date with Bruno. She didn't need to go through that. If her mother called later, let her find out.

Her mother talked about what a pain in the ass her father had been lately. She asked whether Joanie had made any progress with the lawyer about Gary. She meant about instituting divorce proceedings and getting some child support in the meantime. Joanie answered with shrugs and grunts and sat there preoccupied until her mother finally left, saying she had things to do.

Yet she went to the window and watched her mother's car back into the street and felt nostalgic for her visit. She caught her reflection in the window glass: an unfriendly face, eyes she didn't recognize.

She made *pasta fagioli* for Todd and left it on the stove. All he'd have to do was warm it up.

She went upstairs to get ready. She was tired, and defeated by her inability to even decide on what to worry about most. She held her hand in front of her to watch it shake and understood she was also a little excited.

In the shower, she gave the conditioner extra time to work. It seemed to make a difference when she was drying her hair. She used a little mascara on her eyes and Coty Softest Pink on her lips. She decided on the black zip-up with the culottes and the pink flowers. She couldn't find her shoes.

She was ready by quarter to six. She went downstairs carefully, like the way she looked could be jarred loose.

Todd was sitting in the kitchen. She walked in and sat down opposite him. He looked at her dress and makeup.

"You see the *pasta fazool*?" she said.

He nodded. She could feel a bleakness gathering around their day. They sat opposite each other with their hands on the table, like cardplayers without cards.

They heard Bruno's car pull in. This was what her life with her son had become, she thought: the two of them sitting in the kitchen, waiting for whatever happened next to happen.

Todd's shirt was dirty. His hair looked like a rat's nest.

Bruno looked great. He stood just inside the back door, like her date for the prom. She let her eyes work from his feet up, the way movie cameramen tried to be tantalizing. He was wearing a granite-colored Italian sports jacket. He was holding a bouquet of yellow roses in a white paper bag. "They were outta the red," he said.

"They're great," she said, getting up. She pulled a vase out of the cabinet for useless stuff and dumped the roses in it with some water.

"How are you?" Bruno said to Todd. Todd sat there at the table with his back straight and his hands folded, as if to say, I'm good.

"Let's go," Bruno said. "We gotta move."

"Where're we going?" Joanie asked. She was trying to arrange the flowers.

It turned out they were going to a B.B. King concert in Hartford. Bruno knew somebody who knew somebody, pulled a few strings at the last minute. First they had to go to the dealership and pick up the tickets; the guy was dropping them off there.

"Why didn't you go pick 'em up from the guy?" Joanie asked.

"He owes me a favor," Bruno said.

They said good-bye to Todd. He was still sitting at the table, the roses spread out in front of him.

"Don't wait up," Bruno said.

"We won't be that late," Joanie said.

But in the car she thought about it: the concert would probably go past eleven, and they had an hour's ride back after that.

"Everybody'll still be there," Bruno said. They climbed the ramp onto I-95. "You can meet the guys. *There's* a treat." She figured he meant at Goewey Buick.

After he merged into traffic, he looked over at her.

"You look very good," he said.

She murmured a compliment back. They went by an old Coppertone ad painted on the side of a building, a little girl's bathing suit bottom pulled down by a terrier. The terrier's head was missing.

Bruno turned the radio on and then off. "Took a long time," he said.

She could see what a big deal this date was for him and she was touched. "Well, you blew your opportunities," she said.

"Ho." He put his hand out. "Let's back up here. Wait a second. I did not blow them. I did not blow them. What opportunities?"

She shrugged. "Oprah says women have ways of

letting you know." Why was she saying this? What was the point of teasing him?

"Where'd you hear that?" he asked.

"Oprah," she said.

"Oprah," he said grimly.

"Oprah knows everything."

"Oprah knows *dick*. Pardon my French."

They got off 95 at the Kings Highway exit. At the bottom of the ramp a woman was peering at the stop sign from a few feet away through a camera with a huge lens.

"This woman's takin' pictures of the stop sign," Bruno said as they pulled up alongside. He looked at Joanie, and she shrugged. He rolled his window down. "Excuse me. What's the interest here?" he asked the woman. She ignored him.

"I'm sure *I* don't know," he said. "I'm sure I can't say." She looked at him briefly and went back to her camera, moving around to get different angles. "Maybe you see something I don't," he said. "Maybe it's me getting jaded. This is possible." He waited for her to say something, and then he drove off.

"You like B.B. King?" he asked her.

She said she did.

At Goewey Buick three or four guys were standing and sitting around waiting for customers. She was introduced. One of them arched his eyebrows when he was shaking her hand and said, "Va-va-va-voom."

"Somebody leave an envelope for me here?" Bruno asked. The guys said Cifulo had it. Cifulo was out. "Maybe he left it in your office," one of them said.

They went to look. His office was partitioned with glass off the showroom floor. While he rummaged through his metal desk Joanie looked around. Someone had pinned a Goewey Buick circular to the bulletin board next to her. She read a correction printed in a box under the headline, OOPS!: "Last week's circular incorrectly states, 'Free leather travel case with any test drive.' The correct copy should read, 'Free daily calendar with any purchase of a Skylark Executive Edition.' "

The office was a mess. There was a big Mr. Coffee on the file cabinet, with a couple of mugs and torn blue packets of Equal around it. The garbage can was spattered with something and piled with little metal-handled Chinese takeout boxes. One still had the chopsticks sticking out of it. She straightened a framed poster with the title MY FIRST MILLION. It was a photograph of stacks of money. "That's the previous guy's," Bruno said when he saw her looking at it. "I never took it down."

One of the guys she'd been introduced to poked his head in while Bruno searched. "Listen," he said.

"The Korean was back. He said you promised him ten percent."

"Yeah, yeah, yeah," Bruno said. He lifted the blotter on his desk and shook it. "Some people say *one* thing, some people say something *else*. The *hell* did he do with those tickets?"

"This guy said he was gonna call the Better Business Bureau. What happens, he comes in with them?"

Bruno pulled one drawer out of his desk and dumped it on the floor. Joanie jumped. "If he does, we deal with that then," he said.

They watched him turn his office upside down.

The guy folded a piece of gum into his mouth. "Cifulo moved two Rivieras yesterday," he said. "He tell you? He said to tell you he was gonna match your totals. He said he was gonna be making that trip with you."

"Tell him not to buy any new luggage," Bruno said, distracted.

"Is that it?" the guy asked. He pointed at an envelope on the floor.

Bruno picked it up, checked inside, looked at the guy, and walked out. Joanie followed.

"Hey," the guy called after him. "You gonna leave your office like this?" Bruno waved, like he'd wished him a good trip.

In the car he said, "Morons."

They were quiet on the way back to the highway. Bruno turned the radio on.

She formulated questions about Joey Distefano.

"So how you been?" Bruno asked.

She searched his expression, but he was watching the road. "I been all right. How good're you gonna be?"

"I don't know. It'd drive me crazy."

She pulled her eyes to her lap. "What would?"

He looked at her. "What do you think? Your husband takin' off."

A police car went by the opposite way, its lights going.

"Lemme ask you something," Bruno said. "He leave you fixed at all for money? It's none of my business, I know."

She shook her head.

He made an exasperated noise. "Joanie, you gotta get after him. The man *owes* you a little bit here."

She nodded.

A Yardbirds song came on. Joanie turned it off.

"You hear from him at all? You think he's comin' back?"

She put her face in her hands. She was suddenly near tears.

"Hey. Whoa. Ho. Sorry. I'm sorry," he said.

She was crying. "This whole thing is so bad," she said.

He flipped his turn signal and threw a look over his shoulder and cut across the right lane to the exit. They bumped down the ramp and pulled over once they reached the stop sign. Someone behind them leaned on the horn and swerved by.

"Hey," he said, and he put his hand to her hair. "I'm here."

She leaned over to him, her head on his shoulder, and cried. "It's all right," he said. He cleared his throat. "It's okay."

She sniffed noisily and got hold of herself. She sat up and straightened her back and took a deep breath. "Sorry," she said. "I'm sorry."

"Hey," he said, meaning, It was nothing.

She was looking at him. It was as if with that "Hey," he had touched a finger to her feelings for him. He kissed her. She put a hand to his throat. She moved her lips, trying to communicate tenderness. He pulled back from the kiss, and his fingers were on her cheek.

She smiled, and thanked him for being sweet. She wiped her face.

"I'm not sweet," he said.

"We should get going." She ran her spread hands

down her thighs like she needed to dry them. "We gonna eat?" She sniffled again and wished for a Kleenex.

He pulled across the street and up the entrance ramp. He said he figured they'd get into Hartford first, get situated. Eat ginzo on Franklin Avenue, a nice place called Carbone's.

When she didn't say anything, he added that the concert wasn't until nine.

"I didn't think that was gonna happen," he said a little while later.

She thought maybe she could press this as an advantage. You are one cold bitch, she thought. She put a hand to her hair, as if to remind him where his hand had been. "So tell me about Joey Distefano," she said.

He made squeaking sounds with his cheek. "He talk to you yet?" he asked.

"Wednesday night," she said. "You were there when we worked it out."

"Ah," Bruno said.

"Bruno," she said. "What is the mystery here? I mean, what is the big deal? You guys all work for the CIA? What?"

"We're fuckin' Russian agents," he said tiredly. "We want Milford's secrets."

"He shows up everywhere. I mean, like today I went to the mall, he was at the mall."

"Stop the presses. Joey Distefano's at the mall. What was he doing at the mall?"

She looked out her window. "How should I know? Eating ice cream," she said.

"*Ho,* boy," Bruno said.

She rubbed her face and settled farther down into her seat. She turned on the radio.

She counted exits. After three she asked, "How long did he know Tommy?"

"Look. Me and him and Tommy, we worked together, okay? We had some things going on the side."

Again they were quiet. But every time she wanted to let it go she pushed herself: what had she come for in the first place?

"You said some money was stolen," she said. "From Tommy. How'd you know that?"

"Joanie," he said. "This is not a fucking joke. This is not *gossip*. You don't need to know this stuff. You understand what I'm sayin'?"

She smoothed each of her eyebrows with her index finger and gave up.

"You been talking to people about this?" he asked. "Hey."

"No," she said. "I haven't been talking to anybody. Not a soul."

They ate at Carbone's. Bruno was preoccupied through all three courses, watching the waiters across the room like they'd already cheated him. She worked her way unhappily through her fettucine *abbacchio*, surprised at herself, because she was still thinking about their kiss and not focused enough on her disappointment at having found out almost nothing.

Bruno left a ten-percent tip. "The guy slopped coffee around like he had Parkinson's," he said when she noticed.

The concert turned out to be outside, at Bushnell Park. Bruno didn't seem to have known that and was unhappy about standing around on a lawn. He kept sneaking looks up at the sky and shaking his head. There were about a thousand people crammed into a space that she figured should hold fifty. Half of them annoyed Bruno. A guy next to her had a baby that kept taking off his Orioles cap and hitting Bruno with it, and a little red puppy on a leash that kept winding and unwinding around their legs. In the crush, they were pressed together. Bruno made a jerky motion and the dog yelped.

Another guy pushed into them holding a little black dog up high, like the dog needed to see. The guy was calling for B.B. It had to be forty-five minutes before the warm-up act.

"Hey. Dan Blocker," Bruno finally said. "He can't hear you, pal." When the guy looked at him he added, "Somebody's lookin' for you over that side of the park," and pointed.

They stayed like that, shoved back and forth by the crowd. She saw Bruno gauging the distance to the street, to see if it was worth the fight to just leave.

Finally there was cheering, and a kid with long blond hair got up onstage and announced the opening act: Alberto.

"What the Christ is Alberto?" Bruno muttered.

Alberto climbed up onstage in black tights and white pancake makeup. He had a red dot rouged on each cheek and black eyebrows painted in a mournful expression. He was carrying an easel and an armful of placards.

"You gotta be kidding me," Bruno said.

Alberto stood up the easel and set a placard on it. The placard read: THE PICNIC. Alberto sat cross-legged onstage and began pulling things from an imaginary box. A flute began to play.

"A mime," Bruno said. "They're opening for B.B. King with a mime."

An old black man twenty feet away stood open-mouthed. "What're you doin', fool?" he called.

Joey Distefano was right behind the old man. He turned when he saw her and disappeared.

"There ain't nothin' in your hands, fool," the old man called out.

"Whatchu doin'?" a black woman behind him called. "You at a *pic*nic? You gonna go hungry."

"Bruno," Joanie said. She had his arm. "He's here. Distefano."

He looked where she was pointing and pushed a guy aside to see more clearly.

She couldn't tell if he was faking shock or not. "Bruno, what's goin' on?" she demanded.

"Where was he? You sure it was him?" He was right in her face.

"This sucks," someone next to her called. "*You* suck."

"Pal," Bruno said to him. "I'm trying to talk here."

The guy gestured to the mime onstage. "What, is he drownin' you out?"

"It was him," Joanie said. "I know it."

He turned without saying anything and pulled her through the crowd.

She excused herself and said she was sorry whenever she could to the people who got shoved as he yanked her along. They were both looking, but with the size of the crowd and the fading light, it was hopeless.

He stopped so that she bumped into him, halfway to the street.

"No big deal," he announced. "You wanta stay? See the concert?"

She gaped at him.

"Or let's go," he said. "We'll grab a movie."

He looked back and forth casually, giving the search one last shot. "What?" he said. He mimicked her open mouth.

She put her hands on her hips, trying to look like she was tired of this nonsense. She had no idea what to make of his actions.

"Has nothing to do with him," Bruno said. "You *like* it out there?"

The crowd roared, and Joanie looked back toward the stage. Alberto's easel had collapsed. He was trying to pick it up, and placards were fanning out from under his arm like an oversized hand of cards. People were shouting out guesses, as if he were still doing mime.

She turned and headed out of the crowd. She had no notion of whether it was toward the car—it probably wasn't—but she couldn't put up with this anymore and was tired of letting Bruno lead.

He caught up with her at the edge of the grass, near a Polish-sausage vendor. He asked if she knew where she was going, and she said she wanted out of Hartford, now. She led him around the park, back to the car. "Nice-lookin' Polish sausage," he said from behind her. Otherwise they didn't talk.

In Meriden she said, "You're not gonna explain anything about what's going on."

That stretch of 91 was dark, and the dashboard lights weren't much help in reading his expression. Every now and then, oncoming headlights swept over him. "I didn't expect to see him up there," he said. "He didn't tell me he was going up there."

"So? What, does he tell you everywhere he goes?"

"Apparently not," Bruno said.

"Is he following me?" Joanie asked.

"Following *you?*" Bruno said. The car lifted and pancaked slightly over a rise, the sensation unpleasant. That sense she'd been suppressing that Bruno already knew what she'd done was coming back.

"You work together," she repeated glumly, as if she couldn't believe he'd saddle her with such a lame story. When he didn't answer, she got frustrated. "When does he work as a cop? Every time I see him he's wanderin' around doin' nothing."

"He's workin' Wednesday night," Bruno said.

It shut her up. She gave the lights outside her

window great attention and tried to systematically run down the ways in which he or they could have possibly guessed what happened. They'd seen her there. They'd seen her near there. He'd seen the damage to the car.

She was trying to calm herself. She pinched her lower lip with her thumb and forefinger.

"We'll go down to New Haven," he said. "They got some nice bars there. Sedate."

She released her lower lip and gave him a single, flat wave, as if to say, Whatever.

But as they approached the New Haven exit she roused herself.

"I'm not sure this baseball game with Todd is a good idea," she said.

"And why is that?" Bruno asked. He sounded bored.

"Because I don't know what you're involved in," she said. "I don't want Todd mixed up in anything."

He didn't answer.

"Don't get off here," she said when he slowed for the exit. "I don't wanna go to a bar. Just take me home."

The car accelerated so smoothly she wasn't sure it had slowed down. "You don't want Todd getting mixed up in anything," he repeated softly. The way he said it chilled her.

She watched the tall highway lights roll by as yellow cones and ovals on the hood.

"Am I gonna have to tell him he can't go?" she asked.

Bruno seemed to be just driving. He opened his mouth wide, stuck his tongue out, and closed it again. She shifted her weight and pulled at the armhole seams of her top.

An image came to her of Gary hiking some trail out west, with the sun on his hair. It made her miserable and angry.

No warning, she thought. How clueless do you have to be to have no warning your husband's about to walk out on you?

I shoulda had more fun, she thought sadly, as if looking back on a life that was over.

The rest of the way home, Bruno sat there like he was alone in the car and she stared morosely out her window.

A block from her house, he pulled into the back of a Laundromat and parked. He rolled down his window a little and the breeze came in and lifted his hair. It was pretty where they were. The streetlight spread the shadows of leaves across the car.

He shifted so his back was against the door and he was facing her. She couldn't see him very well. Her stomach had that unsettled caffeine-y feeling. She

waited for him to say something. She touched the tip
of her tongue to her upper lip.

Something prowled across the parking lot, in the
distance. She guessed raccoon.

"Lean forward," he said. "I wanna show you
something."

When she did he touched his finger to her bottom
lip. She opened her mouth slightly.

He took her hair between his fingers and turned
them gently and pulled her farther forward. Their
noses grazed. She could smell a faint scent she hadn't
noticed before, his shaving cream, maybe. He turned
his head slowly to hers and kissed her. She was conscious of the awkwardness of her pose and of breathing very slightly. Late in the kiss, he outlined her
upper and lower lips with his tongue.

She kissed the side of his mouth, and then his
cheek, and eased back.

They sat there, a foot or so apart. Because of the
brightness of some areas under the streetlight, her
eyes weren't getting very used to the dark. "Come
over my house," he said.

She kissed him again, a little kiss.

"You don't wanta come over my house," he said
quietly.

She looked down and shrugged, and then looked
back at him, unsure if he could even see her.

He put his hands on both sides of her head, pulling her hair outward. She could feel it fall to her ears. "Tell me if you want to. Open up to me only if you want to. You don't want to open up, don't open up," he said.

"Like you open up to me," she said.

"Hey. This is *business*. This is what business is. People taking *care* of themselves. The freedom of the individual to fuckin' make somethin' of himself. Am I out of line on this?"

She eased sideways against the seat, a more comfortable position.

He ran his hands over his face. "Whaddyou think time it is?" he asked.

She didn't know. A car turned around in the parking lot and its headlights blinded them.

He sighed. "Knowing what the fuck you're talking about. It's rare, Joanie. So rare."

She put her hand to her mouth. She wanted to kiss him again. Do you have *any idea* what you're doing? she thought. She shifted all the way around and sat back against her door.

"How're you doin' for money, really?" he said out of the darkness.

She pulled a leg up onto the seat between them and folded it under her. "We're all right," she said warily.

"I think you got a little more ready cash than you think you do," he said.

She felt saliva in her mouth, and she swallowed so that he could probably hear it. Something ticked in the dashboard. "Where?" she said. "You know something I don't?" She tried to sound jaunty.

Some kids rode by on bikes, circling and screeching. They swerved near the car, and one of them lost his balance and thumped it with his hand. The sound seemed to come from her chest. They cut through the parking lot to the street. Each of them banged the dumpster on the other side of the lot on the way past.

"*Where?*" Bruno said. "I'm talkin' about Mr. Gary. Who's probably got a steady job, a little something stashed away, a coupla bucks nobody's touched?"

She didn't know what to say, or if that was what he was really getting at.

He held up one finger. "We never know until we ask. What's the worst that can happen when we ask? What's the *worst* that can happen?"

He seemed to be waiting for an answer. She cleared her throat and swallowed again.

"You know what the hard part is?" he asked. He waited. "Am I coming through out there?"

"What's the hard part?" she said. She sounded scared.

"The hard part is doing it. Doing anything."

She sniffed. "Obviously."

"Obviously my ass. My ass, obviously."

"I don't even know what we're talking about here," she said.

His head leaned forward in the darkness. "You say, I am going to do this. That's what we're talking about. Otherwise you wander around—you know what you do? You wander around in *thrall* to somebody. That's what you do. You're in somebody else's fucking *thrall*."

Her face and stomach felt as if she were going down in an elevator. Her neck prickled. "What if he's not willing to do what I want?" she asked.

"Then you know what you do? You do something to hurt him," Bruno said softly. "Where he lives."

PART THREE

TODD

LAST NIGHT I watched a movie called *I'll Take Sweden* with Bob Hope and then one called *Boeing Boeing* with Tony Curtis. They were both terrible.

Audrey got sick again and I cleaned it up, but you can still see the spot. I don't know what's wrong with her.

I tried calling my Dad by using Information in these cities: Spokane, Seattle, Olympia, Tacoma, Yakima, Walla Walla, Sacramento, Redding, Chico, Eureka, Santa Rosa, Yuba City, Crescent City, Denver, Durango, Boulder, Buena Vista, Fort Collins, Greeley, Grand Junction, Glenwood Springs, Steamboat Springs, Pagosa Springs. A lot of them I found in an atlas of his called *These United States*. If you call the regular operator and give the city and state, they'll give you the area code.

I have a map where I put a pin in the city after I call.

When my father was still here, one of the things he liked to do was go to Yankee and Met games. We went like twice a year. He went to the World Series in 1986, when the Mets played the Red Sox, and saw the ball go through Bill Buckner's legs. I don't know how he got tickets. He had friends. He said he wanted to take me, but I was only four and my mother thought I was too young. She said she didn't think I would have even remembered going. I would have remembered.

He threw the ball around with me a lot. When he threw me ground balls, he called me Luis, after Luis Aparicio, a player he liked when he was a kid. I looked him up in Bill James's *Baseball Abstract*. He's in the Hall of Fame.

I called the police again and hung up again. I'm never going to do anything with that. I might as well just stop.

My mom came back at one in the morning from her date with Bruno. I don't know how long the concert was supposed to go, but I doubt it was that long.

Last night I had a dream so bad I don't even want to talk about it.

Toward the end, Sister Justine came into it. Sister

Justine last year was one of the ones who'd watch us during Mass to make sure we were singing the songs right. Sometimes kids would make up their own words to try and crack you up. Sisters hate that.

Sometimes you really didn't know the words, though, and you didn't bother reading along in the Missalettes. She came down the row once and grabbed me by the elbow, and I didn't even know what I did wrong. I was singing, " 'Oh, my soul, praise Him, for He is our health and salvation. Christ the high priest bids us all join in His feast, victims with Him on the altar,' " and I thought those were the right words. She scared me.

At the end of the day on Monday, she made us all keep our seats and she announced that Todd Muhlberg was going to sing a hymn the right way for us and we were all going to listen to the right way before we went home. She kept the class after, because I didn't know the words. This made me even more popular.

She made me go up to the front of the room. She picked a different song and she didn't let me use the Missalette. I don't know why she picked a different song. Maybe she figured I might have practiced the other one.

Then, when she had me up there, she made me wait until there was perfect silence.

I remember standing there with my hands folded, everybody looking at me, everybody ready to go. Their schoolbags were all on their desks.

She made me sing the whole thing. She made me repeat one part of it, because I messed it up. And the whole time I was singing I was looking at her, and here's what I was thinking: I was thinking, You're not making me a better person; you're making me a worse person. I felt better, thinking that. What she made me sing still goes through my head at weird times:

> *For the sheep the Lamb has bled,*
> *sinless, in the sinner's stead.*
> *Christ the Lord is risen on high.*
> *Now He lives, no more to die.*

BRUNO

HERE'SA KINDA JOBS I had when I was a kid, these
other guys were out with their seven iron at Fairchild-
Wheeler: Laying asphalt. Spreading asphalt. Humping dirt for road crews, that whole Route 8 extension.
Passivating. You want to see a shit job: this is a job
people don't even *do* anymore. Now they got ma-
chines, and they gotta replace *those* every few years.
I was however old, twenty-two, I finally got hooked
on at Vadnais Metals over on East Main Street, the
first day I'm there the guy I'm supposed to report to
doesn't know what to do with me. Big, red-faced
Polack; always looked like whatever you asked him
was funny. Mr. Kuntz, I gotta take a leak. That's
funny? Mr. Kuntz, where do I punch out? That's
funny? I'm there bright and early Monday morning,
got on new wool pants 'cause my uncle says, Light
work. Mr. Kuntz is baffled. Mr. Kuntz has never

heard of me. He says to the guy he's with, We could put him on the passivator, and they give each other these looks, and I go, Oh, shit.

They take me down like seven levels of cellars. I'm thinking, Oh, this is lovely. We come to this concrete room, I can't describe it. For light, there's one bulb, handmade, Thomas Edison. Nothing on the walls. It's a huge holding area where all these hollow metal cabinets are piling up. The size of small refrigerators, hollow, soldered together. One side of the room is this big stainless-steel pit, like a giant sink. Two feet deep, ten or twelve feet around. Drain in the middle. There's a Puerto Rican in rubber hip boots and rubber gloves in the pit. He's got this wand in his hand, wired to a portable generator. There are these big plastic tubs with screw-on tops next to him. One says WATER. One says HYDROCHLORIC ACID.

The Puerto Rican is introduced to me. The voices in there with the metal and the concrete, you can't hear anything. Hector's wearing safety glasses and his clothes are dotted with yellow, like somebody exploded a mustard bottle in front of him. There's a little vent fan in the ceiling.

Here's the drill: Vadnais Metals is making its own metal cabinets, for who knows what. They solder the things together, the solder discolors the metal. They show me, with one of the cabinets waiting to be done.

Even in the bad light I can see it: the little rainbow patterns around the joint, like the sun on oily water. That has to come off. Since it's stainless steel, nobody's sanding anything. What you do is you find some guys on the bottom of the food chain, Puerto Ricans from Father Panik Village or guineas from Kissuth Street who don't know any better, and you show them how it's done. How it's done is these guys take a wand that's charged with juice from the portable generators and they wrap the wands with gauze and rubber bands. Then they dip them into the hydrochloric acid. Then they swab the discoloration. Then the discoloration goes away, magic. Then they rinse off the cabinet with water. Then they do it again.

Except the electricity breaks down the gauze. So you gotta keep rewrapping the wand. And to do that you gotta take off your rubber gloves. And you rinse your hands afterwards but the acid doesn't feel like anything until a minute goes by, and then it feels slick, and then it burns. And the acid eats through the rubber. And stuff gets sprayed around. And the fumes are a solid thing pressing into your face.

Just standing there, I was leaning back from the fumes. I said, Hey, turn on the *vent,* and Hector said, the first thing he said to me, It's on.

I'm looking at this and I go to Mr. Kuntz, When do I start? and he goes, Start now. I go, In these? and put my hands on both sides of these new wool pants. Pathetic.

The headaches. The burns, when the shit got down into your gloves between your fingers. You'd go to rub your eye and you'd think, *Oh. Very* nice. *That* wasn't close, was it?

They left me there, that first day. I heard the door shut and heard them go all the way up the stairs. They were metal stairs. Near the top, Mr. Kuntz said something and the other guy roared. Laughed so hard he had to stop on the stairs to get his breath. Hector went on without me for a little while. The first thing I did was fold up the cuffs on my pants. I remember realizing this Puerto Rican felt sorry for me.

He showed me how to get into the clammy rubber waders, how to check the gloves for prior damage. Everything that was wet, I thought, Acid. It was nine-twenty-five. I already had a headache from the fumes. I pulled over my first cabinet. It flexed and boomed with that sheet-metal sound. There was nowhere for the sound to go. Hector hit the light cord tipping his cabinet over, and it circled our heads, swinging shadows around like we were in a mad scientist's lab.

Those wool pants that first day had the ass eaten out of them. My shorts underneath were yellow and mealy, like wet Kleenex. You could roll pieces off them with your fingers. I punched out that day with a hole in my pants, like somebody in a vaudeville show. I stood there and punched out. My ass was cold. It was funny to Mr. Kuntz and funny to everyone else. Get a load of this, you gotta see this. Standing there at the time clock looking for his card, a wop with his ass hanging out.

Hector got moved out after three weeks, complaining of headaches. The day Hector left, I went upstairs and said, Hey, I got headaches, too. Mr. Kuntz said, Hey, kid, I got prostate. Sally's got a drinking problem. Hermie's got a stutter. What do you want from me? Two weeks after that I had to stay out a day, I got acid in my eye, the son of a bitch fired me, no questions asked. I had nothing, twenty-two years old, I'm holding my hand on my ass.

I run into a lotta women attracted to me, it's the same story: Bruno, there's something different about you, I don't know why I'm so interested. Bruno, I'm thirty-five years old, unmarried. I live with my mother, she's a burden on me, I'm not unattractive, I still have my looks. Bruno, I never know what you're thinking. Meanwhile, their eyes: they'd hate me if they could.

Love. Everybody's thinking about love.

Two years after that job, I drove up to the University of Hartford and found the dorm where Mr. Kuntz's daughter was a college coed. Eighteen years old, small ass, bobbed hair, in her room she did stretching exercises, legs out to here. They locked the dorms at eleven o'clock, but that was a joke. Her room was on the fourth floor. She left her fire-escape windows open.

I sat on the top landing by some storage rooms and listened to their stereos. Neil Young. Jackson Browne. Two hours of pissing and moaning: "Oh, Lonesome Me." One by one, the rooms shut down under me; I could feel it. It was three, four o'clock. The security guy, probably a hundred and four, went by in his little cart. I wanted a disguise that was an insult. I punched two holes in a grocery bag and tore a smiley face in it. I tied it around my neck with my tie. I went down the fire escape.

I stood at her bed and waited for her to roll over, that's how sound a sleeper she was. When she was on her back I put my hand on her mouth and she woke up. She understood not to scream. She got out of bed and squatted in a corner of the room. This all took a very short time. She was still holding the edge of her quilt. She dragged it all across the floor. She didn't even look eighteen, with the light from the window. I didn't rape her. I made her take me in her mouth.

JOANIE

WE USED TO GET assigned saints and martyrs to read
and think about for a week, and the girls always got
assigned girls who were martyred because they refused to do something impure. The stories were never
clear on what. Usually the Romans were involved.
The most they'd tell you was that so-and-so wanted
to ravish her. I imagined a woman lying back on a
sofa with her arms behind her head. After that I drew
a blank. They were always clear as to what happened
after she refused. We weren't sure what the Romans
wanted in the first place, but we were real clear on
what happened when you didn't give it to them.

The stories always ended the same way: the guys
doing the terrible things and killing were amazed to
see, as St. Whoever checked out, that her expression
was so calm. Sometimes she blessed them. Sometimes
they'd convert right there. I liked to think about them

feeling bad afterward. Those girls were heroes, the stories would end up, because their spirit had conquered their flesh. But it always seemed to us they were heroes because their spirit had conquered the *guys'* flesh. You heard only that the girls had had something *they* had to overcome.

When Bruno dropped me off and I came into the kitchen, Todd was still in his chair, like he hadn't moved in six hours. I asked him what he was still doing up, and he said, "Nina called. I told her where you were."

He went to bed while I was brushing my teeth. Standing there at the sink, I said, "You gonna say good night?" And he said, "Good night."

It was hot, and I lay there in bed and tented the covers. The catechism always talked about duels between the spirit and the flesh—bad news for me, because one I knew was strong; the other I wasn't so sure about.

We always thought: something out there was so bad it was better to have boiling oil poured down your throat. It was better to have your hands cut off and fed to dogs in front of you. What was it? We were dying to know.

They told us about sins of the flesh way before they told us about sex. Sins of the flesh were almost irresistible, and that was the end of the subject. You couldn't think of a better way to keep our attention on something. It wasn't all our fault. It was all sexy, all of it. Grace, sin, martyrs, everything. Protestants didn't get that: they had a cross with nobody on it.

But it made us independent. All this talk about guys and how out of control they were and what you had to protect: at least it meant we weren't on the bottom.

It gave us some distance. To this day, sometimes I think the hardest part about sex is keeping a straight face.

There are a lot of good things you get out of being Catholic. It's just the hard way to get them.

Back then, we were thinking, Suppose the Romans came for us? The thought crossing your mind: that wasn't a mortal sin. That was the devil tempting you. You were supposed to fight it. The trick was how long it had to be in your mind before it was a mortal sin: Five seconds? Thirty seconds? Two minutes? Then we thought, Was worrying about it the same as thinking about it?

Mortal sin sent you to Hell forever and venial sins sent you to Purgatory. There weren't too many venial sins on sex. They tended to go to mortal right away. So we'd lie in bed or, worse, kneel there in church and think those thoughts, and remember that not only did mortal sins send us to Hell; they also pounded nails into Christ's body. You saw a lot of girls looking up at the crucifix, ashamed.

I was up all night the night Bruno dropped me off. I ended up sitting at the living-room window.

When they talked about sex and the devil tempting us, what they never figured out, or maybe they did, was that we weren't worried about the devil; we were worried about ourselves. I always imagined God facing me after I died, and going, Don't try and blame this on the devil. *You* were the one who wanted to think about it, weren't you?

Nina

THIRTY-THREE YEARS she's been around men, she hasn't come close to figuring them out yet. Not close. She married one of them when someone with the brains of a squirrel coulda seen he was a washout first time he walked into the house. Stood around in his little bicycle-racing outfit, mad at her because she was gonna make him late. He sold commercial time for TV, so he was supposed to be a big shot. With me it was like, Mrs. Mucherino, how are you? How's the family? Like that was the way you got around Italians, you talked about their family. He was snapping at her even then. She said, "Ma, he's under a lot of pressure." Who's not under pressure? She said, "Ma, he feels bad about it, too." So what? How many years, he was mad at the way he treated her, he took it out on her?

So she gets hurt. She won't do nothing about it; she won't try and force the *stugazz* to help support his own kid. So at least he's gone, right? How much trouble can she get into, then? Few months later, she's running around with Mr. Bacigalupe himself. What am I supposed to say to her? How stupid can you be?

You talk; they don't listen. I talked till I was blue in the face about the *cavone* she went with after high school, Lawrence. Next to him, Bruno looked good. Dirty, with the long hair and who knew what else, no job, no ambition, what a mouth he had on him. I heard twice from Lucia that he was telling the neighborhood what Joanie would and wouldn't do. I told her: he's not coming around this house anymore. You're gonna go off and meet him under a bridge somewhere or in the park I can't stop you, but he's not coming here. Ooo, that guy. I hated him so much I hated the saint he was named after. I heard after they broke up that Bruno beat him up so bad he put him in the hospital. I know this: I ran into him a month later, he had his fingers in a splint; he wanted nothing to do with me.

I warned her a thousand times about Bruno. She knows him better than I do. And I sit there and talk and it's like talking to the wall. Her eyes are out the window, on the dog, everywhere but me. I tell her, Joanie, I'm only looking out for you. I'm not telling you this for *my* benefit.

It's like she thinks that what's behind her is gone, so she can either choose this or get nothing.

I asked Sandro to talk to her. He's her father, he should talk to her. I wait for him to think of it, I'll be ninety-nine years old.

He thinks I worry too much. Whatever it is, I worry too much. He still thinks the other one is coming back.

I told him: Civil War songs are coming back. Soupy Sales is coming back. Your mother, God rest her soul, is coming back.

That was the end of that discussion.

The first one, as far as I was concerned, was the kind of nightmare with no surprises. You marry Gary, you know exactly what you're getting yourself into. Bruno I didn't even want to think about.

Oh, was I wild when I heard Joanie was out with him. I called to ask if she wanted to see a movie, Todd tells me she's out on a date with Bruno. I said, *Bruno*. Don't think that little stinker didn't know what he was doing. Sandro gave up trying to calm me down. But he's been working on me since: What good's it gonna do to come in her house yelling? What good's it done up to this point? Why not surprise her and not push it and try to work on her that way?

I'm her mother. I'm supposed to be looking out for her. I want to tell her to get a life, a real life. Though I don't know what I'd say if she said back, Ma. Get yourself one.

Todd dreamed about the time he was almost hit by the car on Margerita Lawn: the slow motion, the pale-blue sky with the one cloud, the horn, the chrome fender. He never told his parents about it. He'd been in third grade and ran across the street to avoid being touched by Lori Malafronte. Lori Malafronte's scream had shocked him. The dream turned into a memory of pushing snow down the curve of a car body, and he woke up feeling guilty.

He could hear Nina downstairs. It was raining. He sat up and swung his legs to the floor. He felt weak and fuzzy. He rubbed his ear until it was hot. He found a sock. It had dog hair on it and an unpleasant damp feel. He listened for arguing but didn't hear anything. His mother'd be mad he told about Bruno. He pulled on the sock and his little toe slid through a hole in the end. He wiggled it and imagined being dead, the Mass said for him. Girls would be crying. His father would be sorry for what he'd done. He imagined funeral bells, the flowers on the altar, people filing in. Maybe he'd been a martyr somehow.

He stood up and stretched with both arms out in front of him, like a water-skier. He wandered over to the window. An animal that looked like a Davy Crockett hat wandered across his yard. A raccoon? Muskrat? Divorce, he thought. Separation. Remarriage. Stepson. By thinking of things you could understand them.

He finished getting dressed and tramped downstairs. "Here he comes," he heard his grandmother say.

He went into the downstairs bathroom instead and stood pointlessly over the toilet, listening to them murmur in the kitchen. The new shower curtain had a surprisingly intense smell that he couldn't track down. Then he could: pool liner. A kid's pool, a wading pool.

"You want coffee?" Nina called from the kitchen. "We made coffee."

"Ma, let the kid take a leak," his mother said.

He flushed the toilet and came into the kitchen. Nina was wearing a white sweat shirt with FBI in big red letters across it. Underneath the red letters it said FULL-BLOODED ITALIAN in little green letters.

His mother gave him a big smile as he sat down.

"What're you smiling at?" he asked.

"Listen to you. What a mouth on you," Nina said.

His mother put an English muffin in the toaster for him. "So, Ma," she said. "You wanna go to this pottery demonstration or not? 'Cause I'm goin'."

"That's terrible," Nina said. "Who'd want to demonstrate against pottery?"

His mother waved her hand once, like there were gnats around, and told her it wasn't that kind of demonstration.

They went on talking. He still didn't have his coffee. He kept feeling he had to wash his face. He imagined he projected a bitter silence, but they didn't seem to be noticing. His grandmother finished a story she'd been telling about an escape artist on the news. They'd put him in a box and put dirt and cement on the box and the box had collapsed and crushed him. Could they imagine? It was horrible.

"How was your date?" he asked his mother.

They both stared at him. The English muffin popped up.

"I don't think that's much of your business," his mother finally said quietly.

He got up and hunted around the cabinets the

way Audrey hunted in the tall grass. He left the muffin where it was.

"You looking for anything, you let me know, now," his mother said.

"I'm gonna go over Brendan's," he said.

"You gonna eat your muffin?" she said.

"No," he said.

"You gonna have any breakfast at all?"

"No." He left the kitchen.

Brendan was still a little pissed at him, but he came around. Todd brought over the lacrosse helmet, and Brendan ignored it. They were sitting in the kitchen and Brendan's mother kept giving Todd sympathetic looks that puzzled and annoyed him. Brendan's little brother, Taylor, was playing guns outside with two friends.

Brendan's mother hunched to look out the window. Across the yard, Taylor was sitting on one friend and beating him on the head with a plastic gun. Brendan's mother called to him and wanted to know why they had to play so violently. Why didn't they play where they didn't shoot anybody?

"How do you play cops and robbers and not shoot anybody?" Taylor called.

His mother looked a little stymied by that. "Why don't you just *question* Mickey?" she finally said.

There was a silence outside, while the kids apparently thought it over. Brendan rolled his eyes at Todd.

"Aw right," Taylor called. Then he said, in a quieter voice, "But if he doesn't listen, then we can *kill* him."

Brendan snorted. Brendan's mother finished cleaning the counter and then she left.

Brendan emptied two packets of presweetened Kool-Aid into two cans of Coke Classic. They could hear his brother making the sound of machine-gun fire outside. They sat there slugging the Cokes.

"I can feel my teeth like dissolving," Todd said.

Brendan nodded. "Isn't it great?"

They walked down to the park near Milford Beach. Todd wanted to tell him what was going on. The rain had stopped and the sun was out. The grass was still wet. Their sneakers were soaked. Todd's were the Nikes his father had bought him, and the soles were separating at the instep.

They sat on two big tree roots and watched little kids play football. They knew one of the kids, a fourth-grader named Woods. Woods was wearing his PEE WEE jersey and his name was sewn on the back upside down, so that it read SPOOM.

"You left the lacrosse helmet at my house," Brendan said. He was wearing a CLYDE THE GLIDE T-shirt that reminded Todd of his JUDGMENT DAY tank top.

"You can hang onto it," Todd said. He never thought he'd get out of the mess he was in, except by some magical luck. He felt the need to be kind while he waited for that to happen, as if the world would recognize it and take care of him.

The kids in the football game ran a sweep. It looked like recess getting out. Both teams milled around for ten yards and fell in a heap. Todd looked over at Brendan's T-shirt every so often, glum about the way everything seemed an ironic reference to his secret.

"I'm goin' to Yankee Stadium tonight," he said. Then he realized it sounded like bragging.

"Yeah?" Brendan asked.

"You coulda come, but we couldn't get another ticket," Todd explained.

Brendan nodded, watching the game. "We got *Ad Altare Dei* tomorrow night," he said.

Woods, with his red PEE WEE jersey, was running toward them. He planted to cut and was piled on from behind. He yelled and got up and hopped around on one leg. Todd flinched, remembering soccer tryouts the year before, his knee twisting with a little *crick* that sounded like someone a few feet away cracking a nut. The sound scared him down to his feet. His father had taken him to the doctor and the doctor had handled his leg casually while he talked, like a length of hose.

"He all right?" Todd said.

It looked like he was. He was walking around on both legs like he had a sliver in his foot. "Remember, before confirmation, when we heard we were gonna get slapped in the face by the bishop?" Brendan said. "And we joked about like a fight breaking out?"

"Or that he'd belt us across the face," Todd said.

"We didn't get anything like that," Brendan said. He ripped up some of the wet grass and piled it on top of his sneakers.

Todd watched Woods stand on one foot and swing his other like it was a pendulum. You're a great son, he thought. Here you're supposed to be so upset about your father leaving and how often do you think of him?

"What's the worst thing you ever confessed?" he asked Brendan.

The ball bounced over to them and Brendan kicked it back with his foot. "I don't know," he said.

"If you did something really terrible, would you confess it?" Todd said.

Brendan looked at him. "Why? You do something? What'd you do?" He sounded enthusiastic.

Todd told him nothing, but by then his face was red and he'd given himself away. Brendan stayed after

him and made fun of him, and when Todd got up
and said he had to get back, Brendan followed behind,
guessing what it could be: Stealing? Sacrilege? Praying
to Satan? It was only after Todd got home and waved
good-bye and repeated that he had to go in, he had
all this stuff he had to do, that he realized that none
of Brendan's guesses were as bad as the real thing.

He sat out in the front yard an hour early, waiting
for Bruno to show up. He had his glove with him
for foul balls. His mother was in the living room with
the window open, on the other side of the screen. In
the afternoon sunlight she was just a shadow that
came and went.

"When's the game start?" she asked.

He shrugged. He was matching Japanese maple
leaves to one another. He'd pulled them off the little
tree she'd planted.

He heard her clunk something around in the living
room. "I'm still not sure this is a good idea," she
muttered.

He checked his wallet. He had only five dollars.

You have enough money?" she asked.

"I have enough money," he said. Across the
driveway, near the telephone pole, sparrows trooped
around on the weedy part of the lawn.

"It's like you're out almost all the time now," his mother complained.

"I'm *not* gonna say anything," he finally said. She left the window.

Bruno's Buick turned onto the street and pulled up the driveway. Bruno got out and flipped him a new Yankees cap. It sailed end over end and landed in the grass. "You wear it," he said. "Me, I'm not committing myself till we have a five-run lead."

He asked if Todd had his glove. Todd held it up. "Joanie?" he called.

He was looking at the side of the house and listening for an answer. Some birds cheeped. "Where's your mother?" he finally said.

Todd said she was in the house.

Bruno looked disturbed at the news. "We're *go*in'. Good-*bye,*" he called. He waited another minute and gestured Todd toward the car. When they got in, he looked like he was deciding something and then started the car. "Your mother mad at me?" he asked as he backed down the driveway. "She say anything to you?"

Todd said she hadn't. After a little while he volunteered, "I don't think she wanted me to go tonight."

"You got that right," Bruno said.

"J'ou eat yet?" he asked a few minutes later.

Todd nodded. He hadn't, though. Why he did stuff like that, he had no idea.

"We'll grab something, anyway," Bruno said.

Todd spread out on the leather seat. It was a dealer car and had the new-car smell.

Bruno yawned so widely his eyes watered. He made a loud chewing noise and straightened up. "When's your birthday?" he asked. "I had a good idea for a present."

"It's already over," Todd said. "May eleventh."

"The eleventh? I was born the eleventh, too."

"The same day?"

"The same day."

They got up on I-95, heading south. Traffic was heavy. "It was like two weeks after my dad left," Todd said.

"Happy birthday," Bruno said.

"Really."

A big red Jeep Cherokee swerved alongside them. The windows were open, and the bass *whoompf* of the stereo was amazing even from there.

"What a day," Bruno sighed.

"You didn't sell anything?" Todd asked.

"It's not the not buying," Bruno said. "It's the bustin' 'em off that gets you."

Todd looked back at the road. He didn't know enough to talk about it.

"One guy today, he comes back in: 'Hey, this Skylark option package you just sold me, I just saw it in the paper a lot cheaper at Valley Motors.' I need these comparison shoppers, right? Next he'll be kicking the tires. I go, 'Valley Motors, jeez, you know, you're welcome to comparison shop with them, but it's only fair to warn you we had some dealings with them, we found some serial numbers filed off, you know what I'm saying?' "

He hit the turn signal, and they headed off the Sears exit in Bridgeport.

"What's that mean?" Todd said.

The Buick rolled down the ramp and stopped at the light. It was idling funny and shook. Bruno pumped the gas. He said the numbers filed off usually meant the cars were stolen. Somebody'd probably hijacked a truckload of new ones and sold them to the dealers.

How could he just tell people that about them? Todd asked. Wouldn't they complain? Bruno said not if it was true. Todd thought about it and asked how he knew it was true.

Bruno shrugged and told him he wasn't getting all the trade secrets tonight. The light changed and he went straight a block and hung a right. He hit the automatic door locks. Someone broke a bottle in an alley they passed.

"Where we goin'?" Todd said.

"Little diner," Bruno said. "You'll like it."

They were in a lousy part of Bridgeport. Todd was still thinking about his story. "Does Valley Motors know you're doing that?" he asked.

Bruno shrugged again. "Hey, the buyer's gonna go, 'Hey, I hear you have stolen cars here'?

"See, what Valley Motors gets, they deserve, because stealin's wrong. Am I right?" Bruno asked. "What'd you, lose your voice?"

"No, it's wrong," Todd said. He was afraid to look up.

It was starting to get dark. They were driving along under the highway. There was nothing around but an abandoned car and a chain-link fence. A page of newspaper rose in the wind and floated in front of them. Todd was getting a clogged feeling in the back of his throat from swallowing so much. "Why're we goin' here?" he asked.

Bruno pulled over next to a concrete highway support that went up into the darkness and out of sight. He cut the engine.

"Why're we stopping?" Todd asked. He had one hand on the seat next to him, the other on the door handle. His glove was on the seat between them.

"I wanna talk, before we get to the diner," Bruno said.

Todd rubbed his face with the flat of his hand and tried not to panic. "Won't we be late for the game?"

"Don't worry about the game."

Todd could hear the traffic high above them. He looked around. He could make out a streetlight opposite the car, but the light on its cross arm was smashed. "Is it safe here?" he asked.

They'd be all right, Bruno said. Nobody was going to touch this car.

Todd asked why not. They heard a noise. Two black kids paraded by, eyeing them. Bruno waited until they were past. Then he settled in his seat, facing Todd. He spoke slowly, like Todd was going to have trouble following. He said, "Here's the deal. I need for you to talk to me about what happened the night you drove home from your confirmation party."

Todd froze. He had four fingers curled around the door handle. His eyes were on the dashboard. The traffic way above his head made a threshing, regular sound.

"The night Tommy Monteleone was killed. I need for you to talk to me about what happened."

Todd made a show of concentrating. He sat forward in his seat. He folded his hands between his thighs as if he were praying.

He looked straight out the windshield in front of him, terrified. He said, "We just drove home."

It was completely quiet. The number changed on the digital clock. Bruno folded his arms, like he was going to try a different tack. "Let me explain something to you," he said in a low voice. "What we're involved with here is a serious thing. A guy was robbed, and he was killed. And I'm giving you an opportunity. What is your opportunity? Your opportunity is the opportunity to *tell* the *truth*."

Todd opened his mouth and Bruno held up one finger. "Don't"—he paused—"tell me something if it's not the truth. The truth is what we're here for. *Capiche?*"

Todd nodded. He was crying. "We just drove home," he said.

"You can help me right some wrongs," Bruno said. He held his index finger and thumb up together in the darkness in front of Todd's face like he was holding a spice for Todd to sniff. "It's *not right* to the guy who was robbed and killed. And it's not right to the other guys who *invested* in him. You hear what I'm sayin'?"

"How do they know there was money?" Todd said.

"What're you *tellin'* me?" Bruno said. As he got angrier Todd got more scared. "You want to see the police records? You want to go *down* see the police records?"

Todd interlocked his fingers in his lap and sniffled. He leaned hard into the door.

"Then what is this 'How do they know' shit? What is that? Where'd you learn that? In *school?*"

"I'm sorry," Todd said. He rolled down his window and rolled it up again. "Is the diner near here that we're goin' to?"

Bruno licked his lower lip and scratched the razor stubble on his chin. Todd could hear it. "You don't want to talk about it," Bruno said. "This is a traumatic thing. This I understand."

"We didn't do anything," Todd said miserably.

"You're what," Bruno said. "You're eleven years old. What do you think's gonna happen to you? It's an accident, you're driving along, bip, there he is. Nothin' you could do. You got out, see if you could help, there was this envelope."

"No," Todd said.

"You tell me, or you tell the cops. You tell me, I tell the cops something else."

Todd wiped his eyes with the heel of his hand.

"You know what I see when I look at Todd? I see a boy who *wavers*. A boy who *vacillates*. This is not the time for vacillation. I know you're saying, Be safe. I'm saying, This is not safe. Do you understand? That's the subject of our evening together: *this* is *not* safe."

Todd swallowed. "We're not goin' to the game, are we?" he said.

"There is no game," Bruno said. "Not for you."

He turned off the dashboard lights. It was now totally dark.

Todd said, "We may a hit something." He didn't recognize his voice. "We stopped, we didn't see anything."

"You may a hit something," Bruno said out of the darkness.

"We may a hit something."

"What're you *telling* me?" Bruno said. "You wouldn't *know*? You see his head? You wanna go down the police station see pictures of his *head*?"

Todd started crying again.

Bruno opened his car door and the overhead light went on. He didn't get out. After the darkness Todd had to shield his eyes with his hand. "I hurt your feelings?" Bruno said. "Is that what I did? I hurt your feelings? Tell me again: you hit somebody by mistake. You tell me that again.''

"I told you," Todd said.

"You tell me again."

"We mighta hit somebody by mistake. We heard a noise. We thought maybe it was a dog or something. We got out, we didn't see anybody."

Bruno nodded. He kept nodding. The door was still open. "You don't respect me," he finally said.

"It's the *truth*."

"Get out of the car."

"Get out of the car?" Todd said.

Bruno leaned across him, scaring him, and opened his door. Todd was already leaning against it and almost fell out. "Get out of the fucking car. You don't respect me, get outta the car. I don't want anything more to do with you."

"How'm I gonna get home?" Todd said.

"Fuck do I care? Walk. Fly," Bruno said. "Take a fucking monorail. Get outta the car. Want me to *get* you outta the car?"

"Wait, wait," Todd pleaded. "We did hit him. We did hit him. We were going along and my mother was driving too fast and we just hit him."

Bruno leaned back across him and shut his door. Then he sat up and waited.

"We stopped and went back, but he was dead. She went back, I didn't go back. We were gonna go for help. I thought she was gonna go for help. But then she didn't, and the cops were there when we came back, and we went home and she called, but she didn't get through."

"She called the police?" Bruno asked.

"She didn't get through. It was busy. I heard it," Todd said. He was still crying.

"And this is the way it happened. Exactly."

"And then we never called again."

"And then somebody found an envelope. Your mother found an envelope."

Todd shook his head.

"Don't *start* with me. Your mother found a fuckin' envelope," Bruno said.

"We *didn't*. I swear."

"The money in that envelope was not all Tommy's. You understand?"

Todd shook his head and hiccuped. He wiped his face.

Bruno sat forward. "Tommy and Joey Distefano and I were *holding* that money." He put his hand out, to show what holding meant. "Holding that money, for some other people. Those people *want* their *money*."

"We didn't find any," Todd said.

Bruno flapped his lower lip with his index finger. It made a light, popping sound. "Your mother went over to Tommy after, but you didn't?"

Todd nodded.

Bruno watched him a minute longer and then started the car. "Aw right, look," he said. "We'll go get somethin' to eat. We'll stay out. Far as your mother knows, we went to the game, you didn't tell me anything. Understand?"

Todd nodded.

"Hey. Am I here all alone? You understand?"

Todd said he understood.

Bruno put the car in gear. They backed over something backing out. They drove to an Arby's in a better part of town and Bruno made him order a big meal even though he wasn't hungry. When the food came, Bruno went to the men's room behind the bar, and when guys came and went and the connecting door swung open, Todd could see him talking to someone on the pay phone.

NINA

OVER THE LAST few months I told her about every possible group I could think of: the Serra Club, the Christian Mothers, the Ladies' Sodality, the CYO, the Rosary Society, the Parish Review Board, the St. Anthony's Women's Society, even the Knights of Columbus. Or it didn't have to be in the Church: there were bus trips I knew about to Atlantic City, to the mills in Fall River, to Broadway shows. Ida What's-her-name ran them out of her house.

I even told her about this martial-arts class they were running at the Bridgeport Y. I figured, you know, a woman alone.

Nothing. She didn't want nothing to do with any of them. Okay, I figured. This Gary thing'd take a while longer.

Instead she ends up with Mr. Bacigalupe.

I took Sandro's advice; I didn't push it. Let her

tell me when she's ready to tell me. So we sat there like *chidrules* and it never came up. I even said, "You got something you wanna talk about?" She said, "No." She was always like that.

I wanna tell her, You get involved with him, I'm wearing black. I'm in mourning. I lost a daughter.

So we're sitting there in the kitchen and she doesn't want to talk about him and she doesn't want to talk about anything else, either. I was telling her about my bursitis, which is awful lately. My shoulder, it absorbs the dampness at night. I feel like a sponge. She's barely listening.

I told her the house looked good and asked if she was having company. She gave me a look like what was I getting at, and I felt like saying, Hey, forget it, let's not talk, let's just sit here, all right?

I asked about Gary, had she heard from him.

I asked about her son.

The dog, we talked about the dog.

Finally, I go, "Joanie, I give up. What do *you* wanna talk about?"

She goes, "Ma, you're not helping any, you know?"

This is what she said to me, after I sat there for thirty-five minutes talking about things she could do to help herself. I felt like saying, Okay, maybe they weren't the best ideas, but I was *trying,* you know? I was trying.

It hurt, what she said.

They think you don't have any feelings at all, that you just come and go without them. We were over Lucia's the other day, she and Todd were outside the whole time. It looked like hell. I asked her if maybe she shouldn't come inside, and she came back at me so fresh I thought, Forget it, and went right back in the house. In front of her son, too.

Then she gets in these moods and it's like, Jeez, Ma, we don't see enough of each other. I just keep my mouth shut; I don't say a word. Every now and then, though, I tell her, When you want something, you have to work at it.

They don't wanna know nothing. They gotta learn the hard way, just like we did.

I can't talk to Sandro about it. The kid's fine. Gary's coming back. She'll work it out. Happy days are here again.

This morning we were sitting there in the break-fast nook, I was going through the mail. The Church was raising money again, like in the old days, for the orphans in the Philippines or Indonesia, the little kids with flies on their noses. And I started getting tears in my eyes. Sandro sitting there, thinking I'm nuts.

And here's the thing: I was crying for myself. I was looking at poor kids who didn't have a pot to piss in and crying for myself, like seeing their faces was making me panic, making me think that there was nothing I could do to get out of my life.

TODD

IN THE TOILET at Arby's I tried to figure out what to do. On the metal wall of the stall there was a sign: IT ISN'T POSSIBLE FOR US TO CLEAN AFTER EACH USE. Somebody scratched out enough letters so it said, IT ISN'T POSSIBLE TO CLEAN AFTER U.

My mother says when I was little and a kid had been beating me up on the playground, she found me one night going to bed with a hammer.

I had time to confess and make it right and I didn't. I had chances. I knew what the right thing was and I did the wrong thing. I had the Sacraments and all this training and I did the wrong thing, and kept doing it.

God's supposed to forgive you if you're sorry. I'm sorry.

Also in the toilet in Arby's I said an Act of Contrition. I got off the toilet to say it.

Someone came into the bathroom and I had to get up. It was an older guy and he gave me a look when I opened the stall door. I don't know what he thought I was doing in there. My knees were wet from the floor. My eyes were like I had an allergy.

Part of me is glad. Glad that someone knows, glad that something's finally going to happen.

My dad'll hear about it in the paper, or maybe from a relative when he calls like a month later.

There was this kid I knew in third grade. He always, always got in trouble. He would only get hit between classes. Sister would take him to the office then, so he wouldn't miss anything. I remember the way, on the days he was in trouble, he spent the whole period at his desk, sitting up straight, his hands folded, waiting.

JOANIE

MY MOTHER AND FATHER argue about directions. They have fights over what's faster, this or that road. Which has more traffic. My mother'll say, Why you going this way? You coulda gone that way. As a kid, I sat in the back and had to listen. Even then I knew they were arguing about this decision instead of the other ones. How they ended up *here*, how they got *here*. Instead of where they ended up in general. I mean with their lives.

My mother's turning into one of those old people who think the rules are going to hell everywhere, the kind who hang around the pool at condos watching for rule violations. Reporting the kids without towels, the kids who do cannonballs.

But then I'll see, like this morning, that she left some stuffed shells for us, wrapped in that careful, housewifey way, and my heart'll go out to her.

I don't want to hurt her about Bruno. When I was with him, it was like my head was saying no but my mouth was saying okay. Which is about the way the two normally operate.

A month or so after Gary left, Todd and I were sitting on the floor in the living room one night, listening to the radio. We were in a kind of stupor. The TV was broken. It was hot, and Todd kept rubbing his forehead with a wristband he was wearing. It reminded me of the summer he was always drying his sweat with a hand towel he carried around. We were listening to an oldies station. They played Petula Clark's "Downtown." Todd hummed along. "Just listen to the rhythm of the gentle bossa nova; You'll be dancing with a—before the night is over." I never knew that word. He sang the last part to himself at the end—" 'Everything's waiting for you' "—and I remember thinking that maybe we'd be all right, maybe we were going to make it.

All these days since the car thing have been the same, like ugly cabins along a swampy lake.

I never tried to be Queen of Heaven, but I did want to be a good woman, a good mother. It turns out I didn't know how.

I wake up every morning with my heart racing, like every day will be the day that things work out, or at least get resolved.

The sisters used to say, You don't get exactly what you pray for, you get what God thinks is best. So I used to figure I might as well just wait for that, anyway.

My mother said to me once, just in passing, impatient about something or other, "Well, when were you *ever* happy?" It stuck with me. I should have said, Easter Mass, when I was little. With my white dress and white gloves. My candy to look forward to, the sun on the lawn in front of the church, the air fresh in my nose, the trees with the birds I didn't know, talking, calling things like Red key, Red key, or else So Soon, So Soon.

What would she have said? She probably would have said, Oh, you weren't even happy then. But I was, I think.

I just want it all to stop. This morning, after Todd went out, I sat on the sofa with his peeled-off sweat shirt, like it was the last warm thing of his I'd touch.

BRUNO

THE WAY TO GET RESPECT is to treat people like dirt. It's surprising how many people hold this view. I'm told this often. People say this to me; I say no. But I'm no professor. Many times I'm wrong. Often I'm wrong.

People surprise you. People disappoint you. Sure, you say to yourself, so-and-so was a disappointment, but this person, *this* person I *know*. And look what happens.

A more dispassionate man would have said, She doesn't respect you. My friends said this.

You have to have the ability to see the facts without being sidetracked by the history. By your expectations. What *are* expectations? Rehearsing your own lack of imagination. Joanie's not *like* that. Joanie'd never *do* that. Please. The Japs would never attack Pearl Harbor. John Hinckley was such a quiet boy.

Distance. What you need is distance.

What you do is you keep clear who your friends are. Who treated who like what.

Altruism is fine. Altruism is sweet. But you have to think of yourself. Because who else is going to?

And here's something else nobody knows: the week before she got married, I sat in her mother's kitchen three nights in a row until two in the morning, four in the morning, later than that. I wanted to know, out of curiosity, Did she think Gary was ready for something like this? Did she think she was? I was telling her over and over, He's a good man. Fine. We know that. All's I'm saying, Is he right for you? And she said, a little sad, but mostly smiling, Bruno, you haven't given up, have you? I said, Forget me. Forget me. I'm talking about us. And she said, There is no us. There's only you.

I kissed her good night that last night. She didn't want to, but that was all there was to it. I had *tears* in my eyes. When I was up close to her, I whispered in her ear. I said, "You know this is wrong." And when I let her go, she said, "Sometimes you gotta do the wrong thing."

This is what she said to me after all our time together.

The morning of the wedding, I went over to see her again. This is how much pride I had. She was doing her hair in her mother's bedroom. Her mother was thrilled I was there. I said I had an emergency message, coming through. All the way up the stairs, she's trailing behind, tugging on my jacket flap. I had to hit her hand away. And I knock and peek into the room, with the mother standing behind me in the hall, and there she is, sitting there in her white already, three hours early, doing nothing, hands in her lap. And she goes, "What are you doing here?" What am I doing here. How many years, Christmas, New Year's, Easter, I been coming over here? How many years I'd come over, I'd spring for something?

Tonight on the phone, Joey said, "That didn't teach you, nothing'll teach you."

He said, "*Now* do you believe me?"

I feel bad sometimes. I know I haven't lived the right way. I know sometimes people got hurt. They'll always be people like me, people who're glad to be the way they are but also think, now and then, that maybe a vaccination somewhere didn't take. Maybe it's that simple. I read once, I think it was Meyer Lansky, he said, Some people just never learn to be good.

Joanie spent the time Todd was gone poking through his room. The dog wandered in to check on her, shouldering the half-closed door open and unhurriedly nosing around before leaving. She waited until the dog was gone and then pulled out everything he had hidden. The box of letters under the board games in the closet (*Phalanx!*, *Goal!*, *Storm at Dieppe*), the little red spiral notebook, the round candy tin his father bought him on their one trip to the Caribbean (Zombies: Coconut Chocolate Clusters). She knew where everything was. She'd found everything cleaning at one time or another.

The candy tin was filled with photos. Bruno mugging for the camera with his hands curled like a movie monster's. Gary with a new ten-speed and long hair, a photo she'd taken when they'd first met. Audrey on the sofa. Audrey under the willow, a tennis ball in her mouth. Gary pushing Audrey down a snow pile in some kind of king-of-the-hill game. A picture her mother took of the three of them at the beach, Gary holding Todd's boogie board and looking off, Todd holding her hand and staring straight at the camera. Gary painting the garage.

Near the bottom of the tin she came across a Polaroid of the three of them and felt a lurch, like she'd stepped on a loose rug. One side of the image was smeared the way Polaroids sometimes got. The photo was three years old. Bruno had taken it, in their kitchen. She and Gary were at the kitchen table, and Todd was standing between them. The overhead light, a fake Tiffany thing, was prominent. Todd was holding a coffee-table book Bruno'd just given him on football called *The Gladiators*. He was looking directly at the camera. Gary was lifting the salt shaker with two fingers and a thumb, and watching her in a sidelong way. He looked unhappy. She had her eyes on the table. Minutes before the picture had been taken, she'd collided with Bruno in the darkened living room. He was coming from the upstairs toilet, she didn't remember why; she'd been going to get something to win an argument. Gary and Todd had been in the kitchen. Bruno had stopped her with his arm after their bump. His fingers had pressed her neck forward. He'd kissed her, softly, like he was putting a daughter to bed, and she'd kissed him.

Now, with the photo on the rug in front of her, seeing after all these years that moment, Gary's face, and Todd's expression, she thought, Had they known?

The door opened downstairs. She shut the lid of the tin and put everything back and just got out of the room by the time Todd hit the bottom of the staircase.

He stood with a hand on the railing, and they looked at each other.

She came down the stairs. He started up them. "I didn't hear you come in," she said. "I didn't hear a car. Audrey didn't bark."

"She doesn't bark for Bruno anymore," he said, like she should know that.

She eased over to let him past. She said, "How was the game?"

He looked at her, and she saw he was near tears. He continued up to his room, and she followed. He climbed onto his bed, and she went over and knelt next to him and took his shoulders and asked him what was wrong.

He was looking past her arm, and his expression changed so much she turned to follow his line of sight.

There was a slightly curled black-and-white photograph on the rug.

"Get outta my room," he said.

"Todd," she said.

"*Get outta my room,*" he howled. He burst into tears. She tried to hug him but he fought her off. Audrey peeked in the door. Joanie got up and held her hands at her sides like they were wet, and then backed out of the room and shut the door behind her.

She pitched into the upstairs bathroom and sat on the toilet and put her face in her hands. "Oh, God," she said.

The phone rang. It kept ringing.

"*Answer* the *phone,*" he shouted. His voice scared her so much she jumped up.

"I'm getting it, I'm getting it," she said.

She ran downstairs and snatched it up.

"I'll tell you, my husband," Nina said. "They're gonna make a movie about him, called *Lights On, Windows Open: The Sandro Mucherino Story*. Oh, how he wastes energy."

"Oh, Jesus," Joanie said.

"How *are* you?" Nina said. "Todd back yet?"

"Ma, I got no time," Joanie said.

"You got no time," her mother said. "I say one sentence, you got no time?"

Joanie put her hand over her eyes while she stood there holding the phone, and pulled downward like she was trying to take off a mask. "Whaddaya want, Ma?"

"I'm tryin' to find out how things went with Mr. Bacigalupe. That's all."

Todd came downstairs and stood next to her. His eyes were wet. His mouth was a straight line and the rest of his face scared her. He stood with his hands on his hips.

"Did you find an envelope there?" he said.

"Hold on a minute, Ma," she said. "What?" she said to Todd. She had her hand over the receiver and felt a pain in her chest.

"When you went out to look at Tommy, after you hit him."

She flinched at the way he put it, at the brutality of his intent. She said, to maintain her poise, "Hold on a minute, Ma. Todd's asking me something here."

She put the receiver against her chest. He had his hand on his hair and was raking his fingers downward, a self-calming strategy she'd seen him use before. "What envelope?" she said. "What are you talking about?"

"*Did you find an envelope?*" he asked.

"*No.* I don't know what you're talking about."

He turned and left. She raised the phone to her ear again. "What's goin' on over there?" Nina asked. "He all right?"

"Ma," Joanie said. She was stretching the phone cord around the kitchen wall to see where he went.

There was a faint buzzing on the line while her mother let the rudeness go.

"You gonna see him some more?" Nina finally asked. "Your friend?"

"I don't know. Ma, it's almost midnight."

"Bacigalupe," her mother said softly.

"Why do you call him that?" she asked, distracted and frantic. She heard something being dragged on the floor upstairs.

"He was the one started using it, not me," Nina said. "You know, Bacigalupe. Bacigalupo. 'Kiss of the wolf.' "

She had the sensation her chest was filling with gravel. She sat, putting a hand out to catch the chair arm.

Upstairs, there was the hollow, wooden, grating sound of a drawer being pulled out.

"I gotta go, Ma," she said. "I'll call tomorrow."

"Don't bother," her mother said, and hung up.

She got hold of herself and hung up the phone. She stood and crossed to the living room and listened.

More drawers were being pulled out. She took the stairs two at a time.

Todd was pulling out the drawers and dumping them on the floor. He'd gotten his father's big suitcase out of the cubbyhole storage off his bedroom and was pitching clothes into it.

"What's this? You're running away?" she asked. She hadn't succeeded in purging the mocking quality from her voice.

"I'm movin' out," he said.

There was a banging at the door downstairs. Todd stopped what he was doing, a sock hanging from his hand. She put her palm on her stomach and tried to breathe out.

The banging resumed: four big bangs. She could hear Audrey jumping and whining and scratching at the door in excitement, but no barking.

She hurried down the stairs. She turned on the outside light. She moved Audrey away from the back door, made sure it was locked, and peeked out.

Bruno was holding up a bottle of champagne. He gave her a grin that showed a lot of teeth.

She hesitated, with her hand on the doorknob. He turned his head, held both hands up, and arched his eyebrows, as if miming exaggeratedly, "It's your move."

"It's late," she said through the door.

"It's early," he called back.

She still had her hand on the knob. "What's the champagne for?" she asked.

"Celebrate," he said.

Audrey spun and leaped in place, whining. Bruno tipped the bottle to his mouth, miming a drink. He made a face like, Mighty good.

She turned the lock. He pushed the door into her and swept into the room. She staggered back a little into the coats and umbrellas hung opposite the door.

The dog leaped up on him, and he lifted a knee and deflected her into the cabinets by the sink. She came at him again, and he conked her on the head with the bottom of the bottle. It sounded like a hammer pounding in a stake. She gave a yelp and flattened.

"Don't," Joanie said.

"I need her all over me right now?" he said. "We love each other. Fine. We love each other. Great. That's established. Time for her to get outta the way."

"You coulda hurt her," Joanie said. She could hear Todd on the stairs and then the creak of the risers as he climbed as quietly as he could back to his room.

Bruno shook the champagne hard a couple of times and set it on the counter. "I was gonna bring you a Slim Jim, too. They had 'em at the checkout, but a colored woman took the last two."

She stood where she was, a few feet from him, frightened at what could come next. Audrey was trying to get to the bump on her head with her front paws, but all she could reach were her snout and ears.

"You see my Windbreaker?" he asked. "I mighta left it here this afternoon."

She swallowed and shrugged. She said, "Well, you left it here, it's here."

"Yeah, that's what *I* thought," he said. He looked around the room like someone deciding if he wanted to buy something.

"Bruno," she said. "It's late."

"Here's what I was thinking," he said. "I was thinking I could come over, we could have a little talk." He sat in a kitchen chair. "You could open up to me."

She stood there, staring at him. Audrey rolled on her back on the linoleum and finally sneezed.

He got up and wheeled into the hallway, through the living room, and up the stairs. She froze for a minute and then ran after him.

"Bruno, what are you doing?" she said, chasing him up the stairs. He wasn't running. "Bruno, what are you doing?"

He leaned his weight into Todd's door as he turned the knob, and boomed it open. Todd was sitting on his bed, surrounded by clothes. He scuttled back against the headboard.

"Bruno—" Joanie said, working up some real anger.

"What's this?" Bruno said. "We're goin' on a trip? Club Med? South Seas? North Pole?"

Nobody answered.

"Atlantic City?"

"We're havin' a fight," Joanie finally said.

"Ah, a family thing," Bruno said. He sat on the bed and pulled a Vikings sweat shirt out from underneath him. "I certainly don't want to get involved in a family thing."

"Mom," Todd said, like a plea.

"Here's what your son told me," Bruno said. "Your son told me you hit and killed Tommy Monteleone."

She looked over at Todd. Their eyes met. She thought with complete clarity that this was the worst thing yet.

"Your son told me that you then got out of the car and went over to him. Your son told me that you probably took the envelope. Your son told me you been fucking me over all this time. Making me a jerk-off. Playing me like a fucking piccolo. That's what your son told me." His voice hadn't gotten any louder, but there was so much rage in it she thought it could float him over the bed.

"No," she said. She had to force air into her diaphragm to be heard.

"I didn't say that," Todd said.

Bruno shrugged. "This is what the kid told me. I didn't necessarily believe it all. I thought, What do they know at that age? No offense. Maybe he made something up. Maybe he got something garbled."

She put her hand out to the wall. It brushed the phone.

"The envelope thing he wasn't sure about," Bruno said.

Downstairs, Audrey shook herself hard, her collar jingling and her ears flopping.

"I think I know what your problem is here," Joanie said.

"*My* problem," Bruno said dangerously. He folded his hands before him like an altar boy. "You think you know what *my* problem is."

He looked up at her. He contemplated her as if he meant to never forget her in that light.

"You gonna be teaching again in the fall?" he asked.

Her mouth fell open. She didn't think she could endure much more of this. "Math and English," she said.

"It's nice there, huh?"

"Better than Blessed Sacrament," she said.

He smiled. "It's a tough racket, teaching." It sounded like he was talking to himself.

"I could use some English myself," he said, a little sadly. "I don't express myself too good. Well. Too well. See what I mean?"

She took a deep, slow breath. She could hear Todd breathing, too.

"You know what you gotta have in this life?" he said. "You gotta have ability. You gotta have luck. You gotta have the balls to arrive at your own conclusions."

"Bruno, what do you want?" she said. "C'mon."

"C'mon?" Bruno said. "Come on?"

"I mean—"

"What am I gonna be, a headline? 'Bruno Found in the River'? 'Bruno Washes Up on the Beach'? Is that what's gonna happen? Because you found some money and you want to hang onto it?"

"I didn't find any money," Joanie said.

"Did you kill Tommy Monteleone?" he asked.

She looked at his shoes. She looked at Todd, but he was looking away. "It was an accident," she said.

"And you lied about that. All along," he said. "All the things we talked about. You watched me go through this all along."

The three of them were quiet. Bruno rubbed his nose slowly with both hands.

"What was I supposed to tell you?" Joanie said in a low voice.

"This was *me,*" Bruno said. "This wasn't the cops, this wasn't your fucking mother. This was me."

She shrugged. She swallowed again.

"I sat there talking with you, thinking we were getting somewhere, and all along you were thinking, What a fucking jerk."

"I wasn't thinking that," Joanie said.

"Get away from me," he said, and she realized she had her hand out to him.

Todd had his arms crossed and was rubbing them with his hands. He cleared his throat. When Bruno looked at him, Joanie watched him try to make himself completely still.

Bruno turned back to her. She would not swallow again, no matter what. "And what about the new washer–dryer?" he said. "You saved your pennies in the piggy bank?"

She was stunned, flustered at having that dragged into it. "Sandro and Nina helped us out with that."

"Sandro and Nina helped you out."

"Yes," she said. "That's the truth."

He smiled again. "The truth."

"The truth."

"You never saw any money?"

"I never saw any money."

He sat there nodding. Todd started breathing again. "Well," Bruno said. He slapped his thigh. "I apologize for the inconvenience."

She watched him closely. "Bruno—" she said skeptically.

"No," he said. "That's what you say, that's what you say. I got no choice but to believe you."

He stood up. He looked around the room at the mess. "Hey, listen," he said. "You ever do decide to leave town, you let me know. I'll help you run a tag sale for all this stuff. We'll split the profits."

"Bruno—" she said.

"Yeah yeah yeah," he said. He headed to the door. He turned. "Todd," he said, and pointed at him. "Be well."

"Are you in trouble?" Joanie asked. She didn't want to extend the conversation, but she had to know. "I mean, does this have to do with the people you work for?"

"Yeah," Bruno said. "The people I work for. Long time ago."

"You and Tommy and Joey Distefano?"

"It was a while ago," Bruno said, almost dreamily. "And Mark Siegler. You remember Mark Siegler?"

She felt sick. "Mark Siegler?" she said. "What happened to Mark Siegler? I thought he had that heart thing."

"He was killed," Bruno said. "In a calamity."

"A calamity?" Joanie whispered. "What kind of calamity?"

"Heart," Bruno said. "Though I think a big pipe before that. Big steel pipe." He left. She heard him going downstairs. She heard Audrey pad into the den in anticipation, getting out of his way.

The back door opened and shut, but she still didn't hear his car. She listened a minute longer and then went to the top of the stairs. It was quiet. She tiptoed down and peered into the kitchen, tipping her body to see down the hall better. Everything was quiet. She crossed to the kitchen window and looked out through the curtains, but she couldn't see anything. His bottle of champagne was on the table, where he'd left it.

She walked to the back door, thinking a horrible joke was about to be played on her. She found it locked. She tested it anyway, and looked out again, both hands on the knob.

Bruno swung into view from the side of the window, and she shrieked and fell back into the coats.

He looked in on her, then held up his hand in a wave and headed off down the driveway.

She slumped to the floor, kicking the shoes and sandals they'd piled there in various directions.

Todd was peeking into the kitchen.

"You all right?" he asked.

She closed her eyes and nodded. She swallowed, as if finally she could. "He scared me," she said.

"Is the door locked?" Todd asked.

She nodded again. She opened her eyes.

"You okay?"

She stood up. She swiped at her rear and thighs, as if she'd been sitting in dirt.

"Maybe we should call somebody," he said in a frightened voice.

She went to the phone and started dialing. When she finished, she looked at the clock. It was twelve-thirty.

Her father answered.

"Dad," she said. She didn't know what to say next.

"You all right?" he asked. She could hear him trying to get his voice back.

"I wake you up?" she said. She suddenly felt stupid.

" 'S all right," he said. "What's up?"

"Mom there?" she asked.

"Hold on," her father said.

They seemed to be fighting over the phone. Joanie couldn't make out what they were saying. She heard a little of her mother's voice.

"Your mother doesn't want to talk to you," her father said.

"Oh— We had a fight," she said, trying to explain. She made a disappointed noise with her tongue.

"Call her back tomorrow. She'll be all right," he said.

She held the receiver near her chin. Her heel was bobbing and she was looking at Todd.

"You sure you're all right?" her father said.

"Yeah. Go back to sleep," she said. "Dad?" she said.

"Yeah?"

"Thanks," she said. She hung up.

She stood looking at Todd in the light from the hallway.

"I'm scared," Todd said.

"We'll be all right," she said. "What's he gonna do?"

"I'm scared," he said. "Let's go over their house. Let's go over there."

She was going to tell him she'd have to call her father back again, but she saw his face, and her heart went out to him. "You wanna go over?" she said.

"Just for tonight," he said.

"Okay," she said. "Brush your teeth and grab a shirt for tomorrow."

He stood staring at her. He was starting to cry again.

"I'm sorry," he said. "I'm sorry I told."

Before she could hug him, he turned and ran from the room.

They'd be all right, she thought. Years from now, she meant. They loved each other too much to not be all right.

She got her toothbrush from the bathroom downstairs and underwear and a T-shirt from her bedroom dresser. She decided against hunting up a little bag, figuring it wasn't that much to carry loose.

"Hurry up," she called, and then regretted it: it probably scared him more.

He came thumping down the stairs two at a time. He had his little green knapsack over his shoulder. "Audrey's comin', right?" he said.

"Sure," she said.

At the back door, she hesitated. Todd's stomach made a noise. Audrey jumped up once, in impatience.

The garage light on the trees over the driveway reminded her of sitting in the car under the streetlight the night before. She peered close to the window on the side he'd surprised her from earlier.

"Ma," Todd said. She looked at him. He had a claw hammer stuck in his Levi's.

She unlocked the door. She opened it. Audrey bodied her way out past their calves and trotted around, making sweeps with her nose.

Joanie led Todd out and down the driveway. The garage was pretty well lighted. There was an intermittent wind.

She heard the jingle of Audrey's collar stop, and when she looked over her shoulder, the dog had raised her head and was looking off down the street. Joanie pulled Todd into the garage, directing him with her hand around the passenger side. As she moved down the car she checked the backseat. She called once for Audrey, got in, checked the backseat again, and then, once Todd was in, locked all the doors and rolled up the windows. Her stomach unknotted a little.

Audrey trotted up and stood her front paws on the driver's-side door. She unlocked it and opened it again, and the dog scrambled in over her and turned awkwardly around between them on the bench seat before settling down.

She turned the key in the ignition. It was like there was no front end to the car.

She sat there turning it.

"What's wrong?" Todd finally said. The amount of fear in his voice was paralyzing.

She checked to see if it was in park. It was.

"He did something to it," Todd said.

She opened the door. "I'm not gonna check it now," she said. "Let's go."

At the front of the garage, Audrey gave a growl and took off around the house. Joanie grabbed Todd's hand and ran for the back door. On the step she fumbled with the key. Todd called to Audrey. Joanie finally maneuvered it into the lock and got them inside and slammed the door and locked it. A second later, Audrey came trotting down the driveway and up to the door. Joanie looked around as much as she could and let the dog in.

"He did something to the car," Todd said. He had his fist over the hammer in his pants, like someone with severe stomach pain. "He did something to the car to keep us here."

"We don't know that," Joanie said.

"Call Grandpa," Todd said. "Call Grandpa."

"Hold it hold it hold it," Joanie said. She was trying to get hold of herself. She turned on the overhead light in the kitchen and sat at the table. She pushed the bottle of champagne farther away from her. "What're we gonna say?" she asked. "The car's not working; we think Bruno's coming to get us?"

She realized she was sweating and felt the dampness along her hairline and in front of her ear. "Anyway, Bruno was just here. And he left. Right?"

That seemed to calm Todd a little.

"And we got Audrey to protect us," she said. "C'mon. We'll check all the doors and windows."

They checked them together, Todd holding his hammer out in front of them like the Olympic torch. He helped her with a sash that was jammed.

They left some lights on downstairs. She led him up to his room and helped him clear the clothes off his bed.

"I'm gonna sleep in my underwear," he said.

He hung his Levi's over the headboard.

"Where's your hammer?" she asked.

"I musta left it downstairs," he said with alarm.

"Don't worry about it now." She didn't want to go downstairs for it alone.

He didn't look much reassured.

"You know what?" she said. "I think I'll snuggle here with you for a while. Is that okay?"

"That's okay," he said. He scooted over.

She hit the light and pulled off her own jeans and climbed under the covers in her T-shirt and underwear. She turned on her side to face him and folded her hands under her cheek. He was looking up at the ceiling.

"See? This isn't bad. This is pretty good," she said, but her voice had every quality of the end of the line.

Her thoughts rose in the dark like faint balloons.

She could hear water dripping into the big bowl she'd mixed tuna in, in the kitchen sink.

She lay there charged up and exhausted. She felt unexceptional and solitary, as tired as a mother who'd played all day with her kid and hadn't tired the kid out yet.

Tommy Monteleone's name stayed with her, like something she could experiment with to hurt herself.

She saw herself before she got married—sitting in the Milford library, with her shoes off and her legs folded under her—and her heart went out to herself in tenderness.

This whole life, she thought. All this pain: didn't she make it herself?

She tried to calm down. She composed a letter to Todd. She composed a letter to Gary. She asked their forgiveness.

She thought of kissing Bruno. She thought of bats rushing out of their caves, sweeping past her and kissing the air over her skin.

She felt her soul opening up in the dark, unfolding sin after sin. In the gloom, she made out the Blessed Virgin statue on the dresser. Mary's eyes regarded her with mild pity. Her own eyes were brimming with tears. A catechism line swam up from somewhere: *God tries over and over again but the sinner will not hear.*

" 'Downtown,' " she sang softly. " 'Things'll be great when you're—downtown.' "

Todd didn't respond. She looked closer to see if he was asleep.

"Mom?" he said. "I still have to leave, I think. I don't think I can stay here anymore."

She closed her eyes and the tears broke down her cheeks. *This,* she thought. This was the worst moment.

It didn't have to be so irreconcilable, she thought. Remember what we have.

There was a far-off whistling.

She controlled her breathing and focused on her hearing.

The whistling died off.

Audrey raised her head from the rug. Her license jingled: she was moving to hear better.

Something cracked outside, like someone snapping a good-sized stick. Joanie's heart started going.

She heard a sound very near the window. It sounded like someone pouring liquid slowly out of a jar. It sounded like someone urinating against the side of the house.

"Ma," Todd said.

"I hear it," she said. "Shhh."

There was a quick, faint popping sound, like someone had snapped a bicycle spoke.

They waited. Audrey woofed. She lowered her head to the rug again.

Joanie heard the whistling again. It was in the yard. She recognized it: "*O Sordato Innamorato.*"

She sat up in bed. "Call the police," she said. "I'm going downstairs." She got to her feet and turned on the little lamp on his bedside table. She climbed back into her jeans.

Todd was moving for the phone. He had a sober and alert expression, like a frightened general.

"I think he's back," she said. She felt as if she could throw up.

He nodded. Nothing seemed surprising now.

He picked up the phone and started dialing. She opened his door wider and hit the light in the hallway.

"*Ma,*" he said, and when she turned he was holding the phone out to her, his eyes large.

"Oh, God," she said.

He let it drop. He scrambled into his Levi's. At the base of the house there was a slow, metallic sound like the soft scrape of a snow shovel on ice.

"C'mon," she whispered. She turned off the light. She had no plan. She thought she'd take him downstairs, try to locate what was going on, and push him out another window or door and run.

She led him down the stairs. She could hear her hand, sweaty, squeaking and skidding on the banister. Audrey stayed in the bedroom, watching them go.

"Audrey, who's down here?" she whispered. The dog kept her chin on the rug.

They waited in the dark at the bottom of the stairs. Most of the blinds were closed, but she went cautiously around the living room, leading Todd, peeking out where she could see.

"My hammer's around here," Todd whispered. "I can't find it."

There was a sliding sound and a small clank from the kitchen. She felt a breeze at the back of her head and a familiar congested feeling of helplessness. "Stay here," she said. She edged down the hall.

They'd left on the small light over the sink. She crept onto the linoleum. Everything was quiet. She headed for the back door. When she passed the spice cabinet, she sniffed vanilla extract. It always smelled to her like heart, like her love for Todd.

From where she was, it looked like the door was still locked. She slid along the cellar door, trying to get brave enough to get close enough to make sure.

She looked back at Todd. He'd gotten as far as

the edge of the kitchen and was squatting all the way down to the floor, the way when he was sick he'd fold himself over on the toilet.

She looked into the sink. Drops of water were falling softly into the brimming bowl.

The cellar door crashed open, knocking her across the room and into the kitchen table. The table went over. She fell on her front on the linoleum. The champagne bottle bounced and rolled into the living room. Todd screamed.

Bruno was standing in the cellarway, holding up her underwear from the car.

"You forgot your things," he said.

She turned on the floor and tried to tell Todd to run, but he was already running down the hallway. Bruno was over her in one long stride and after him. She got up and chased them. Bruno caught him on the stairs and dragged him down by the legs, Todd's torso and head bouncing as he came down each riser. Audrey was up and barking in an uproar. Joanie punched and tried to kick, and Bruno let go of one leg and forearmed her across the head so that she pinwheeled over a low chair in the living room and landed on the rug. Something shot through her back.

She pulled herself up on an elbow, stunned. She heard a heavy thump and a high-pitched bark from

Audrey. Bruno dragged Todd into the room by the feet and dumped him on the floor beside the coffee table. Then she heard him hustle the dog through the kitchen by the collar and pitch her down the stairs. There was a spectacular crash.

He came back into the living room and stood over them, breathing hard.

Audrey was barking and crying in the basement, and Joanie could hear her dragging herself around, but her voice was getting weaker. Bruno ran his hand over his hair. He flexed his shoulders to fix his shirt. He waited until there was only one solitary bark. Then he turned on the lamp and took a seat on the couch.

Todd was up on his elbows, too. His nose was bleeding. He was crying, but he wiped his face fiercely.

Bruno was looking into her eyes. " '*Sordo come una compana*,' " he said. " 'My stone-deaf love.' "

There was a stabbing pain in her shoulder blade when she tried to put weight on her other elbow. She cried out.

"Pretty good tumble you took," Bruno remarked.

"*Fucker*," Todd said. It was the first time she'd heard him use the word.

"Fuckin' Flyin' Wallenda," Bruno said.

"What're you *do*ing?" she said. "What do you *want* from us? We don't have your money."

He put his hand out flat toward her. "Forget the money. The money's history. Did I ask about the money? The money's over. Please. Let's talk about you."

She went faint and cold and momentarily had the impression she couldn't make out the color of the rug.

Todd was sniffling and got to his hands and knees. Bruno put a foot on his rear and pushed him over.

"Let me tell you a little secret," Bruno said. "Tommy was coming to meet us that night. He parked a mile or so up the road. We were far away and had a bad angle on it, but we saw him get hit. It was pretty dark but we saw some of the car. We saw someone get out."

Joanie remembered the darkened parked car right before the accident. She leaned more on one elbow and pulled her other arm closer to her body to lessen the pain. "Why didn't you do something?" she asked.

"How did *we* know what was goin' down?" Bruno said. "The people whose money we had were already a little upset."

"You knew then?" Joanie said. "You knew then it was me?"

He shook his head. "Not until I saw you again. Saw the two a you again. You're not exactly fuckin' archcriminals."

He stood up and leaned the brass floor lamp at a forty-five-degree angle between the sofa and the floor. The neck of the lamp assembly was on the arm of the sofa. He kicked through it and the lamp part snapped off. He picked up what was left, the rod and base, and wrapped the electric cord around it. Her insides seized up and then released. "Why didn't you do something then?" she whispered.

"Fuck you," Bruno said.

He unscrewed the base and yanked the cord out of the rod. What was left in his hands was about three feet long and hollow and an inch thick.

"Now, what Joey's up to, I don't know," he said. "He was up in Hartford with us, I know that. This I took to be a bad sign. But I'm in deep shit. You understand me? I'm up to my fucking ears."

"We don't have the money," she said.

"Nobody else can have it, Joanie," he said matter-of-factly. "Where else could it fuckin' go?"

"Maybe it blew away," she said. "Maybe the cops took it."

He snorted.

"Think of it like having a overdue book out of the library," he said. "Having a *real expensive* book out of the library. And a real cranky librarian." He stood up. He hefted the brass rod. "Where is it?"

"We don't know," she said.

He brought the rod down on Todd's backside. Todd howled.

"You son of a *bitch*," she screamed. He stepped across Todd and put a foot on her bad shoulder and pinned her. The pain spiraled through her, and she saw lights.

He stood back off her shoulder. When she opened her eyes, Todd was on his side, curled and holding himself.

"What am I gonna do with you?" Bruno asked, like he was talking to a dog that was resisting being house-trained. "What am I gonna do?"

"I can't believe you hit him like that," she said. She was whimpering from the pain and the shock.

"Deal with it," he said.

Rage flooded her and she thought, I'm not sitting still for this, goddamit, and she rocked forward. The pain was blinding. She got more upright, though.

"You think maybe now I should be convinced of your sincerity and I should just go away, maybe with a heartfelt apology. Right?" Bruno said. "Is that what you'd like?"

She looked at him with hatred and nodded.

"That's very nice," he said. "That's nice to know. Now here's some news for you: *I give a fuck*."

"You son of a—" she said, and he hit her again, a baseball swing, in the ribs. He hit Todd across the thigh.

She thought, I have to kill him. He's going to kill *us*.

"Ask yourself," Bruno said. "Why did you do this? Say: why did I do this?"

"I'll kill you," she managed to say.

"You did it because it was me, didn't you, Joanie? Because you had me so far on the fuckin' hook. 'What's *Bruno* gonna do about it? The sappy *fuck*.' "

He hit her again.

She shook. She crossed her arms. She tasted blood in her mouth.

"Ah, you're gonna go all the way to the end, aren't you, Joanie? You're gonna go down with me, aren't you?" he said.

Joanie opened her eyes and could see he was leaning closer.

"Joanie remembers from Blessed Sacrament: martyrs get the crown," he said. "All those saints, Joanie, huh? All they had to do was die."

"Maybe he never had it," she said.

He leaned even closer. He was only inches from

her face. "We searched his house," he whispered. "We searched everything."

She closed her eyes and ground the back of her head into the rug. He had her bad arm. The pain was like someone sawing a wire through her shoulder socket.

"All that time," Bruno said. "You know what I was waiting for? I was waiting for you to tell me the truth."

He got closer still.

"What did you want from me?" he whispered. "What did you ever want from me?"

"Oh, God, oh, God," she said.

"What you did to me," he whispered. "After all I felt about you." She saw tears in his eyes through her own. Todd was on his knees behind him and swung the champagne bottle by the neck, and the sound it made on Bruno's temple was new, was nothing she'd heard before. He made a guttural noise, like a fishbone was caught back in his throat, and he went over. And she had the brass rod in her hands, and Todd had the bottle, and in agony and together they pulled themselves over him and fell on him, as if their retribution were absolution. As if for now it was the only grace imaginable.